“Why don’t you come over to my house for dinner tomorrow night?” she asked.

“What time?”

“Five? Are you working?”

“Not tomorrow. Five it is. What should I bring?”

“Nothing. Just an appetite.”

“You’re a very demanding woman,” he said, letting his arm drop to make room for her to get in the Jeep.

“Just wait till you meet my daughter.”

Chuckling, he closed the door and walked around to the driver’s side. Maybe, just maybe, he’d get her talking. Once she trusted him completely, she would feel safer. As those thoughts came to him, the guilt set in again. What if she didn’t know anything as he suspected much of the time? She would be hurt when she found out who he really was.

* * *

Colton 911: Chicago—Love and danger come alive in the Windy City...

* * *

If you’re on Twitter, tell us what you think of Harlequin Romantic Suspense! #harlequinromsuspense

Dear Reader,

I am sure everyone is glad 2020 is over and hoping for a much better 2021! The good thing about COVID (if anything good can be said about that) is we are all spending more time at home, which for many of us means...more time for reading!

I had the absolute pleasure of writing the second book in part two of the Colton 911 series. I love that Harlequin does twelve books in a single Colton series. They are so much fun to write and read.

My characters fall in love with each other and a five-year-old who is always by their sides. Maya is a sweet, adorable little girl who is deaf, and I hope all of you love her like I do. You met her in part one with January and Sean's story. I am honored to carry on this heartwarming tale.

Stay safe, my avid romance readers,

Jennie

COLTON 911: TEMPTATION UNDERCOVER

Jennifer Morey

HARLEQUIN
ROMANTIC SUSPENSE

Special thanks and acknowledgment are given to
Jennifer Morey for her contribution to
the Colton 911: Chicago miniseries.

Recycling programs
for this product may
not exist in your area.

ISBN-13: 978-1-335-75937-5

Colton 911: Temptation Undercover

This edition published by arrangement with Harlequin Books S.A.

For questions and comments about the quality of this book, please contact us at CustomerService@Harlequin.com.

Harlequin Enterprises ULC
22 Adelaide St. West, 40th Floor
Toronto, Ontario M5H 4E3, Canada
www.Harlequin.com

Printed in U.S.A.

Two-time RITA® Award nominee and Golden Quill award winner **Jennifer Morey** writes single-title contemporary romance and page-turning romantic suspense. She has a geology degree and has managed export programs in compliance with the International Traffic in Arms Regulations (ITAR) for the aerospace industry. She lives at the foot of the Rocky Mountains in Denver, Colorado, and loves to hear from readers through her website, jennifermorey.com, or Facebook.

Books by Jennifer Morey

Harlequin Romantic Suspense

Cold Case Detectives

A Wanted Man
Justice Hunter
Cold Case Recruit
Taming Deputy Harlow
Runaway Heiress
Hometown Detective
Cold Case Manhunt
Her P.I. Protector

Colton 911: Chicago

Colton 911: Temptation Undercover

The Coltons of Mustang Valley

Colton Family Bodyguard

Visit Jennifer's Author Profile page at Harlequin.com, or jennifermorey.com, for more titles.

To Allie, my ever-faithful Australian shepherd,
who gives us big smiles or furry hugs and
a few well-placed kisses

Chapter 1

While not the big-box elegance of a chain bookstore, Mostly Books had its own charm. Rows of new and old books spread across three-quarters of the space, and the coffee counter with three small tables and a quaint seating area took up the rest in the front. Ruby Duarte rang up an order for a gray-haired woman. Her coworker, Melvin, got busy making the iced latte. It was usually just the two of them working the morning shift.

Having taken care of five patrons, all but the gray-haired woman enjoying their coffee in the seating area and one of the tables, Ruby moved to the corner of the counter that faced the windows. She liked watching people passing by, going about their day. A woman and her young child walked along the sidewalk in shorts and summer tops. An early August day in a suburb of Chicago, it was shaping up to be hot and muggy.

The bell above the door jingled, and a man stepped inside. He was dark-haired and a touch over six feet tall—and vaguely resembled her ex, Kid Mercer. For an instant she stiffened, and her heart flew into a panic until she reminded herself that the man couldn't be Kid because Kid was dead. Other than his height, the man's similarity to Kid ended. Kid's hair was lighter, and this man had brown eyes. Ruby had to admit her ex still haunted her.

She breathed through her nose relaxing her nerves. The man wasn't Kid, but that didn't mean one of his associates wouldn't come searching for her. She was always on alert for that.

Ruby went to the register and took the man's order. As she worked, the bell jingled again, and this time a familiar face entered. She was again struck by his good looks, a tall drink of Chris Hemsworth, dark blond hair a bit long and ragged, closely trimmed beard and hazel-green eyes magnetized her. He even walked like the sexy man. His mouth crooked up when he saw her. He came in almost every day before he started his shift at the Foxhole pub down the street.

So far they had only exchanged small talk and hadn't really gotten to know each other. They talked weather and current news and things that happened while he bartended and the goings-on at the Mostly Books store. He seemed nice, though. She had a good vibe about him. That didn't mean she'd let her guard down. She'd just escaped a dangerous relationship and wasn't about to put herself through anything like that ever again. She'd had a good vibe about Kid, too, and look where that had gotten her.

"Hi," he greeted in that deep voice that always tickled her soul.

"Hi yourself."

Last time he had joked with her about his lack of a green thumb and that he'd bought a plant to reassure himself that he was capable of taking care of a living thing other than himself.

"How's the plant?" she asked.

"Not dead."

She smiled.

"I think it's growing," he added.

"That's a good sign."

She had asked him where he lived, and he said in an apartment above the Foxhole. The Foxhole was a fairly upscale pub, but she'd heard some questionable people frequented the place.

"Maybe I'm dad material after all," he said.

Ruby thought of Maya, her five-year-old daughter, and wondered if she would ever want him to meet her. She was extremely protective of Maya, especially since her daughter had finally adjusted to living with her and not the girl's father. Ruby had made great progress with her, and the therapy helped ease the tension in the girl. It broke her heart knowing what Maya must have gone through living with a criminal like Kid Mercer. Although Ruby had never given up trying to get her daughter back, Kid had too many dangerous men surrounding him, and she couldn't get close enough to snatch her.

"Coffee?" she asked Damon.

As always, he ordered a plain black coffee.

"Working the lunch shift today?" she asked as she processed the transaction, keeping the talk neutral between them. He was earlier than usual.

"Actually, no. I have the day off," he said, leaning an elbow on the higher counter next to the pay area.

"Oh, out on the town today?"

"Not exactly. What time do you get off work?"

Her heart did a little flop of excitement. Was he going to ask her out on a *date*?

"Two."

"Would you like to go have ice cream with me?"

She looked outside at the steamy day. She did like ice cream, and she could get something with fudge. And being curious about this man who had come in so many times, she'd like to get to know him more. It was high time she had some fun, anyway, and she wasn't due to pick up Maya until after class tonight.

"Okay."

He grinned. "Great. I'll be back at two. We can walk there, so you don't have to worry about getting into a strange man's car."

He wasn't exactly a stranger. She knew his name was Damon Jones, and he knew hers. They knew some details about each other but nothing too personal.

Melvin handed Damon his coffee. A fiftysomething man with kind blue eyes, Melvin was a humble soul who loved the outdoors. Ruby thought he should work for the forest service rather than serve coffee. He told her once he liked the social aspect of his job.

Damon took the cup and looked at Ruby. "See you soon."

"Looking forward to it." She smiled, and he grinned back flirtatiously.

She watched him leavc the store, glad he didn't see her check out his fit butt in those light blue jeans.

"He finally asked you out, huh?" Melvin asked.

Ruby became aware of him next to her, so caught up in her Chris Hemsworth–fantasy man that she hadn't noticed.

"I guess so. If you call having ice cream a date," she said.

"Oh, it's a date all right, and about time. He's taken it really slow with you. He's been coming here, what—six months now?"

It had been about that long. Damon said he'd been working at the Foxhole pub for the last nine months. And he had taken things slow, something she appreciated. She didn't know if hc had done that for himself or for her. Ruby could be rather transparent, something that worked against her at times.

"Yes."

"I was beginning to think he'd never ask," Melvin said.

He'd been paying that much attention? Another customer arrived, and it was a while before the afternoon slowed. She hadn't stopped thinking about Damon.

At two, she went to the bathroom to tidy herself up. When she emerged, Damon stood inside the entrance, waiting. He saw her and grinned. She smiled back, feeling so good about this. Damon was a good man. She just knew it. Things were finally looking up for her.

* * *

Damon had two primary objectives in his DEA undercover case. One, get to know Ruby Duarte, and two, infiltrate her ex-boyfriend's criminal syndicate. Kid Mercer had frequented the Foxhole, holding meetings there with his followers. Damon sometimes heard them discuss problems with drug-trafficking routes. They hadn't known he listened, of course. Mercer had been a dangerous man with many followers, more than Damon could count. His syndicate had been enormous in the Chicago underworld and still wasn't completely dismantled.

Damon had spent the first three months watching Ruby, getting to know her routines and work and school schedules. Then he began going to the bookstore that also served as a coffee shop, initially not saying anything to her except *thank you*. Over the last four months, he had gradually worked up a friendly rapport with her. He had immediately sensed extreme guardedness in her, which is why he was taking things slow.

He had caught on to an underlying attraction to him, as attested by her occasional nervousness. She had begun flirting back with him after about two months. He had gotten her to reveal a little about herself, even though he already knew pretty much everything about her. She lived in the Woodlawn area, where he also had a house. She was twenty-six, and he was twenty-nine. She liked people-watching. She was going to nursing school. He avoided talking about past relationships because once he asked if she'd ever been married, and she had responded with a curt *no*. The subject clearly was sensitive for her.

Now she walked toward him, dark wavy hair down from her ponytail and light brown eyes twinkling with attraction.

He held the door for her, and they began walking down the street.

"How was the rest of your day?" he asked.

"Uneventful. It always slows down after around noon."

Today he would stop carrying on the small talk. Early on he had joked with her, saying she must love books to be surrounded by them every day. She had said she did, but she was going to school to become a nurse. He had told her he worked as a bartender down the street.

"How is nursing school?" he asked.

"Good. I have a long way to go, but it's good."

"Where do you go?"

"Chicago State University. I had help in getting a grant, otherwise I don't think I could have afforded it," she said. "And I know I couldn't do it without my mother. She watches Maya while I work and go to school."

"Maya?" He knew about her daughter, but they hadn't talked about her in his role as a bartender.

"My daughter." Ruby beamed maternal love and pride. "She's five."

"An adorable age."

Ruby laughed a little. "Most of the time. She can be a real pistol when she wants her way."

They walked in silence a while before she asked, "Do you like kids?"

"I love kids. Hope to have some of my own someday."

That seemed to please her, her eyes smiling and lips curved up slightly. "Maya is deaf."

"Really?" He feigned surprise.

"Yes. Since she was two. I had to learn sign language. She does really well. She learns quickly. My smart girl." She smiled.

"Can she read lips?" he asked.

"She's getting better at that, but lip reading is challenging at best."

"Does she get by okay?"

"She does fine. She is strong and makes friends with other kids. I don't think it will hold her back in life."

"Maybe she takes after her mother."

She smiled again. "She might be a little tougher than me."

Reaching the ice cream shop, Damon held the door for her again. They ordered and took their containers of peanut parfaits to a table. Damon sat across from Ruby, realizing he must be rusty with dating. He had been so involved with his work that he hadn't dated in a long time, long before starting his undercover job here. At a loss for words being with this remarkable, beautiful woman, he ate a few bites, looking at her every once in a while, noting the details. How her eyes sparkled, her tan skin radiated her beauty. She was tall for a woman, too, probably five-eight. And slender.

"So, Mr. Jones, tell me about yourself. How'd you wind up bartending?"

"Damon. I thought it was cool after high school."

"You never wanted to go to college?"

He really did not like lying to her. He decided to tell a partial truth. "I make a good living bartending, and I meet lots of people."

She didn't seem satisfied with his answer, as though she wondered if he had no aspirations in life. Did she not respect a man who held a job as a bartender?

"If you did go to college, what would you study?" she finally asked.

He debated telling her another partial truth. What would it hurt? He pretended to think a bit.

"Criminal justice."

She smiled. "That's a far cry from bartending. Why criminal justice?"

"When I was a kid I was fascinated by superheroes. Getting the bad guys." That was the truth. Growing up with a father like his, he had wanted to be the opposite of what Erik Colton represented.

"Did your parents encourage you to go to college?" she asked.

"My mother died when I was seven, and my father wasn't around much, so no, I wasn't encouraged by them."

"Oh. I'm so sorry. My father died when I was ten. It's hard to lose a parent when you're a kid."

"Yes. My dad's ex-wife raised me, and she did encourage me. She was a good mother to me." He felt good about not lying. He would just avoid saying names.

"Do you have any brothers and sisters?" she asked.

"I have two older brothers, one is my half brother." He'd refrain from going into detail about his newly discovered cousins and all the affairs that had produced other children. They were the children of his grandfather Dean's twin sons from his first marriage. Damon's grandmother, Carin, was always after a way to hoard money. Her latest scheme exposed a claim to the Dean Colton fortune. She had somehow produced a will that named Erik and Axel Colton rightful heirs. Damon had never felt close with her and, as with his father Erik, had a strained relationship with her. He had never felt a need to obtain wealth, just satisfaction in what he did with his life.

"Why wasn't your dad around much?" Ruby asked.

He couldn't say much about that without risking his undercover investigation. "Let's just say he wasn't dad material."

"He had an affair with your mother?" Ruby asked.

That was a delicate question. "Yes."

Ruby turned her attention back to her ice cream.

"What about you?" he asked. "Tell me about your family."

She swallowed a bite and looked at him. "I have an older sister and brother. We stay in touch."

"They aren't from around here?" he asked.

"Wisconsin."

"You're a Wisconsin girl? What brought you to Chicago?"

"I moved here with my boyfriend," she said, and got a faraway look.

She must be referring to Kid Mercer. "Is that your daughter's father?"

She nodded, obviously not happy to be discussing this. Her eyes avoided his, and she seemed to withdraw.

"Is he involved in your daughter's life?" he asked.

Ruby shook her head. “He died.”

“Oh. I’m sorry…”

“Don’t be.” She pushed her ice cream aside. “I should go pick up Maya.”

It was only three. She said earlier she had until five.

“I’m sorry. I didn’t know you don’t like talking about him,” Damon said.

“It’s all right. It is a mood-changer, though.” She smiled, albeit forced.

“Is your family still in Wisconsin?”

“My mother is here. She moved here shortly after I did, and that makes Chicago home.”

She must be close to her mother. Seeing she still wanted to leave, Damon didn’t try to keep her any longer. “I’d like to take you out again, maybe for dinner,” he said.

She smiled, although the residual distaste over bringing up her ex still lingered. Actually, *distaste* wasn’t the right word. *Apprehension* was more appropriate. She was afraid. As well she should be. Mercer was dead, but his band of criminals weren’t.

“I’d like that,” she said.

Damon was both elated and filled with guilt over misleading her the way he was. He had way too much interest in her. He had a job to do, and yet, this felt like a real date. When he should be pretending, he didn’t have to. Honestly, he felt attracted to her the moment he met her. He thought he could keep that under control, but now, being with her like this, he worried he wouldn’t be able to. What was worse? Pretending or not? Either way, the day would come when she’d learn his true identity. She'd be hurt. And so would he, if he allowed any feelings to grow.

He walked with her back down the street.

"Have you been following that story about the Coltons?" she asked.

She did so to make conversation, but she had no idea the bombshell she had just dropped on him. Luckily, the media didn't focus on Damon and his brothers. They focused on Erik and Axel Colton, and Carin, of course. So far. Damon wasn't in the limelight while he worked undercover, and his brothers were more concerned over the damage Carin would cause if her suit were successful. Damon himself was curious of his new cousins and had no interest in taking anything from them.

"No, not really," he said.

"They have cousins they never knew about, and Dean Colton's mistress from way back when is going after their inheritance."

"Sounds like an evening soap opera," he joked.

Ruby laughed. "Money attracts all sorts, apparently."

"I'll say."

"Money was never that important to me. I was more interested in finding someone I could be happy with. I mean, everybody needs money to survive, and I don't want to be the one who struggles to live comfortably, but it doesn't have to be in excess."

"I couldn't agree more," he said, having had similar thoughts about his father and grandmother. He felt a bond grow between them, as though they were magically linked in this moment. And the attraction he had so far been able to temper began to slip from his grasp.

They reached the bookstore, and Damon faced her.

"I'm glad we did this," she said.

"Me, too." The urge to kiss her overcame him. It should be a tactical move, but seeing her full lips and eyes that no longer held that haunted look, he'd do it for more than that. He couldn't deny it. Managing to restrain himself, he kept it chaste and leaned in for a kiss on her cheek.

Getting a whiff of her sweet scent and being so close to her beautiful eyes, something changed in an instant. He could see the heat go into the way she looked up at him. He shifted just a bit and pressed his mouth to hers. Soft at first, the lightning-fast reaction in him and what he felt in her response made him kiss her harder.

Ruby slid her hand up his chest to the back of his neck and kissed him with equal fervor. A few seconds later, she began to withdraw.

Stepping back, she put her hand to her mouth and stared.

"Yeah," he said. "I wasn't expecting that, either." What an understatement. They were explosive together. How was he supposed to conduct his investigation with that kind of knowledge?

After a few seconds, she lowered her hand and pointed toward the bookstore. "Now I really need to go."

"Yeah. Good idea." In a few more seconds he'd be doing his best to take her home with him.

"M-my car is parked in the back."

"I'll walk you there." Although it was still afternoon, he didn't like the idea of her alone in the back of the building, which was essentially an alley.

"No, no." She briefly waved her hand. "I'll be fine." With her palm toward the sky and eyes going up, she said, "Daylight."

He chuckled. "Sorry. Chivalry isn't dead for me." And it wasn't. He just needed to meet a woman who appreciated that about him. Or, at the very least, recognition that it wasn't an attempt to rob her of her independence but, rather, respect her for her exquisite beauty, inside and out.

Damon had given up trying to find that a long time ago, but it was still nice to fantasize.

"It is for most men," she said, smiling.

Still grinning, he said, "Dinner tomorrow night?"

"How about Friday? I have class tomorrow night."

"Okay. You want to give me your address so I can pick you up?"

"Pick me up here."

She still didn't trust him. He could deal with that. "Seven," he said.

"Seven it is."

She smiled and breathed a few deep breaths. He felt the same, still breathless. What would happen after dinner on Friday…?

Snapping out of that fantasy, he remembered Mercer's followers. Ruby wasn't aware of Damon's knowledge of the danger she could be in.

"I'll walk you to your car," he said.

Her smile warmed, obviously touched by his show of what she perceived as chivalry.

They walked in silence with enticement charging

the air. Too soon, they reached her car door. She faced him.

"Well," she said, "until Friday."

"Not unless I come get my coffee in the morning," he said.

She breathed a short laugh, one full of sexual awareness.

Things would be a lot different now. Their acquaintance had gone from platonic to a wide-open road of possibilities.

"Thanks for walking me to my car." Still smiling, she got into the driver's seat and looked at him as she started the engine.

Damon stuffed his hands into his pockets and couldn't subdue an answering grin, knowing it was flirtatious and revealed how good he felt because of her, because of being with her the way he had been this afternoon.

She lifted a hand in farewell, and he took his right hand out to answer. He stood there for several seconds, long after she disappeared down the street. Turmoil churned in his guts. These feelings were too strong after just one innocent date. He was undercover, and she was his primary target for gaining the upper hand on Mercer's criminal followers. The two would surely clash into an unfavorable ending—for him and for Ruby.

Chapter 2

Damon had taken Ruby to the movies once and dinner twice. Now he took her to Matthiessen State Park, about an hour-and-a-half drive from Chicago. He planned on a picnic and maybe a hike afterward. People who weren't from Chicago probably would never guess there was a place with beautiful rock formations, trees and wildlife a relatively short drive away. Growing up in Wisconsin, she and her family would take vacations up north. Her grandparents had a house on Long Lake. This place reminded her of that.

Reaching the picnic area, Ruby helped Damon spread a tablecloth and unload the cooler and a bag he used in lieu of a basket. The table was secluded in trees, and she could hear a stream nearby. A careful look around and she could see water through branches and undergrowth. A path had been trampled down where others had gone to partake in the beauty or perhaps fish. The path where they had just walked was visible but about fifty yards away. She could see people passing by, but this was a private place.

"Have you been to this spot before?" she asked. How had he known to bring her to this table?

"I did some reading and got a map. A very friendly park ranger told me about this table," he said.

"It's so beautiful." And so much more special with him. Their dates had progressively drawn her closer to him, or at the least, much more interested in taking this further. She sensed he felt the same. One could never be sure at this stage of a relationship, however. What she felt might not have the same meaning to him. And she had vowed never to let her guard down until she was 100 percent certain she was with the right man.

"What did you make us?" Ruby had never been with a man who prepared her food. Kid had either taken her out or brought food in.

"Club sandwiches with avocado, chips, coleslaw and fruit," he said, handing her a paper plate with a wrapped sandwich. "Nothing extravagant."

Extravagant enough for her. The gesture was what counted. She took out two sodas and the coleslaw. The coleslaw had come from a deli, but the clubs were homemade. He grinned. "I'm not a very good cook."

Laughing lightly, she sat on the bench across from him.

Eating a bite of the delicious sandwich, she said, "You're an excellent club-sandwich chef."

"Thanks. Just don't ask for anything gourmet." He chuckled at her teasing.

"I bet you could follow a recipe if you had to." Anybody could do that.

Content just being with him, Ruby took in her surroundings, listening to birds and the stream and feeling a soft, warm breeze under a clear blue sky.

"I haven't been to a place like this in so long," she said.

"What other places does this remind you of?"

"My grandparents had a house on Long Lake in Wisconsin. We used to go there all the time. Then my dad died, and everything changed. My mother took us there but not as often. She was pretty heartbroken. We all had a hard time getting past that."

"What happened to him?" Damon asked.

"He got brain cancer," she said. "Brain cancer is ruthless and indiscriminate. We found out, and he lived less than a year. None of us had time to process his illness, and then he was gone. Just gone." Ruby shook her head slowly and looked out across the park, remembering how terrible the whole ordeal had been.

"That must have been awful," he said. "I'm sorry." He reached over and put his hand over hers.

She met his eyes, appreciating the gesture. The *I'm sorry*s never helped. His touch did.

"We seem to have loss in common," he said. "Not the connection I'd prefer, but…"

"You mean your mother?" she asked.

"Yes. She was alive and well one moment, and in an instant, she collapsed and died," he said. "I don't know what's worse, having time to struggle through a terminal diagnosis or losing someone close to you quickly."

"I don't, either. I suppose I'd have to think of the person who is about to die. Going quickly, they don't suffer."

"They also don't have time to get their affairs in order. I would hate to leave things unsettled for my family to deal with."

"I think it would be easier if none of us had to die at all," she said with a smile.

He chuckled. "Immortality, never aging." He nodded. "Yeah. I could do that."

They ate in silencc awhile.

"Where are you from in Wisconsin?" Damon asked.

"A little town called Neenah."

"And your mother followed you here?"

"Yes. She lives with me now. Having Maya around rcally helps her. She loves being a grandmother," Ruby said. "She never had any interest in remarrying."

"Some people get it right the first time," he said.

"They did. My sister and brother and I had a really great childhood up until my dad died. I have so many fond memories. My parents never argued. They talked things through. They were strict but not overly so. They wanted us all to be disciplined and develop good life habits."

Damon fell silent, and she sensed he didn't like talking about his childhood. "Do you have any good memories?"

"Sure. My brothers and I were close. We did a lot together. Rode bikes. Played sports. We were ordinary boys."

"Have you ever been married?" she asked.

"No. My father and uncle taught me how to get it wrong. I don't plan on doing that."

Ruby liked the sound of that.

"What happened with Maya's father?" he asked.

Why was he so interested in that? Was he being cautious and only wanted to know why they ended? Or did he have another motive?

"Why do you want to know?" she asked.

Lowering his head, he looked contrite when he met her eyes again. "Sorry. Just curious, I guess."

"Curious?" He seemed more than curious. He seemed to want details, and that she could not give him.

"Yes. I can see it's upsetting to you," he said. "But I don't want to push you. Really. I'm sorry."

After studying his face a while and unable to determine if he was being genuine, Ruby stood. "We're done with lunch, right? How about that hike you promised?" She forced a smile.

Damon stared at her for a few seconds. "Yeah. Sure. Let's put all this away and go for a hike."

Ruby felt a flash of guilt. Did he deserve an explanation? She was beginning to have very strong feelings for him. If he was as good and decent as she sensed, she didn't want to blow it. But talking about Kid reminded her of how terrified she had been when she was with him and how afraid she'd been of his friends. Damon must see her fear. She was beginning to feel obligated to tell him about her ex-boyfriend, Maya's father, which was absurd because she didn't have to tell him anything. She was just getting to know him.

Maybe she just needed more time. And more time with Damon appealed to her no small amount.

Damon walked beside Ruby in a state of frustration and guilt.

His personal feelings for her were seriously interfering with his ability to conduct his investigation. He had spent so much time trying to melt her defenses, and yet she showed no signs of softening. And more and more, he was becoming convinced she didn't know enough to be worth all of this effort. He also worried his efforts were too personal and not in the best interest of the undercover case.

While he suspected Ruby didn't know anything about Kid's operation, he had to be sure. He was getting pressure from his boss to move the case forward and to do that he needed to determine if in fact Ruby did know something. In order to do that, he needed to know more about her relationship with Kid. He needed to get her talking.

As they hiked along the path, passing rock formations and trees, Damon struggled to find a way to broach the subject of Kid again. She got so upset every time he tried, he wondered if he should let it go and not push as he'd said earlier. But this investigation was going nowhere as long as she refused to open up about the creep. He stopped walking, making her do the same. He put his hands on her shoulders. "Ruby, I know you don't like talking about your ex, but it makes me wonder why. Can you at least tell me why?" he asked.

After looking past his shoulders a while, she finally said, "I just don't like talking about him."

That wasn't enough. He already knew that. "But why, Ruby?"

"He wasn't a good man."

"In what way? Was he abusive?"

"Please don't ask me about him anymore."

"I just want to know about him," Damon said.

"Well, I don't want anyone to know about him. He almost ruined my life. And Maya's. I'm glad he isn't around anymore."

"What happened to him?"

Ruby's lips pursed, and she turned back toward the direction they had come. "I'd like to go home now."

Damn. He'd pushed her too hard. Or had he? She was always so reluctant to talk about Kid. Vague, even. Why? The only logical answer was fear. Someone had to make her face her issue with the man.

He caught up to her. "I can see you're afraid, Ruby. That's why I can't let it go. I'm concerned about you."

Ruby stopped, and they faced each other again. She seemed to search his face for some kind of sign. What was it? That he was being honest? Thankfully, he was.

"Don't be. I'm all right."

He angled his head dubiously, raising his brow in a lighthearted way.

She smiled slightly. "As long as people don't keep asking me about Kid, I'll be all right."

That wasn't what he wanted to hear. "I don't mean to upset you. I don't mean to keep badgering you. But you should talk about him, what happened between you. It might help you, not hurt you."

"I'm not ready for that," she said.

What she didn't say was she wasn't ready for that *with him.*

"Fair enough, but that's not going to make me stop worrying about you," he said. "I've grown to care about you, Ruby."

Her eyes softened even more. "I care about you, too."

He heard the truth in her voice and already knew the truth had tumbled out of him. A warm energy mingled between them. He saw it in her eyes and the tiny curve to her lips. He felt the same reaction in him.

Taking her hand, he walked with her down the path, glancing over at her and catching her own glances.

Back at Damon's Jeep, he began to feel letdown that this day would now come to an end. They had already loaded the picnic supplies in the back. He opened the door for her, but put his hands on the frame to stop her from getting in.

She tipped her head up and faced him.

He put two fingers under her chin, seeing her eyes flare with surprise and heat.

"There's only one thing that will finish this day to perfection," he said.

"What's that?" She played along. She must know what he intended and wasn't resisting.

"This," he murmured, leaning in for a brief, soft kiss. But what he meant to be brief lasted many seconds. The world around him dropped away. All he felt were Ruby's warm, soft lips against his.

When he would have probed for more, he drew back. Baby steps with this one, he reminded himself.

She stared up at him for a timeless moment before she seemed to drift back down to earth.

She patted his chest once, lightly, nervously. "I wasn't sure I was going to do this today, but now I think I will."

"Do what?" he asked. "Kiss again?" He grinned.

"No." She didn't smile. "I want you to meet Maya."

Now, that was progress. "I'd love that."

"I should warn you…she's an excellent judge of character," Ruby said.

"I should pass the test, no problem," he said.

"I hope so." She briefly bit her lower lip. "Why don't you come over to my house for dinner tomorrow night?"

"What time?"

"Five? Are you working?"

"Not tomorrow. Five it is. What should I bring?"

"Nothing. Just an appetite."

"You're a very demanding woman," he said, letting his arm drop to make room for her to get in the Jeep.

"Just wait till you meet my daughter."

Chuckling, he closed the door and walked around to the driver's side. Maybe, just maybe, he'd get her talking. Once she trusted him completely, she would feel safer. As those thoughts came to him, the guilt set in again. What if she didn't know anything as he suspected much of the time? She would be hurt when she found out who he really was.

Ruby wasn't sure what troubled her more: her inability to talk about Kid, or Damon's persistent interest in the topic. He said he was concerned about her.

She believed that. She was concerned about herself and Maya. But she just didn't feel comfortable talking about Kid. First, she was embarrassed at having gotten involved with a man like that. Second, getting pregnant had been an accident. She had used birth control but still got pregnant. Third, he was a scary, dangerous man with lots of men who followed him and thought she knew more than she did.

Leaving the state had been an option, but Ruby had refused to run. She liked Chicago. Maya was settled here and safe. Ruby's mother liked it here. They were close to Wisconsin and could visit family often, but she would not run.

Her mother knew all about Kid and agreed with her. Bethany, or Bette as those close to her called her, had the stamina and strength of a mama grizzly. Something Ruby had inherited—despite her inherent transparency—and Maya had as well. A tiny mite, Maya showed signs of that spirit even at her young age. Ruby was so proud.

"What's got you all smiles?"

Ruby stopped chopping vegetables for the salad to see her mother walk into the kitchen. The house was actually rented in her mother's name, a tactic to protect Ruby and Maya. So far, they had not had any uninvited visitors.

Bette always wore colorful clothes, flowing and figure-slimming. Her dark hair was cut short. She had dark eyes and smooth, olive skin. Ruby had gotten her hair and skin from her mother and her light brown eyes from her father.

"Hi, Mom." Ruby leaned over and kissed her mother on the cheek.

"Can I help?"

Ruby had a big cutting board on the kitchen island and a bowl she was gradually filling with vegetables.

"The grill needs to be lit and the ribs seasoned," Ruby said. "I have water warming for the corn. Baked beans and a salad, and we are ready for an all-American dinner."

"Sounds lovely. Where is Maya?"

"Your cute little granddaughter is in her room playing with her dolls."

"I'll start the grill and go get her."

Just then, the doorbell rang. Ruby stopped chopping carrots.

"I'll get that first," Bette said.

Ruby resumed chopping, but her heart skipped a few beats. This evening would change the course of her future. She just knew it. Having a man she trusted meet her precious daughter was no small event. Damon didn't know how important this was to her, how much of a privilege Ruby considered this to be. Maybe after tonight, he would.

Not many things made Damon nervous, but he was right now. This evening could take his relationship with Ruby into much deeper intimacy. Meeting her daughter meant a lot. He was going to get to know her family. Would this entwine him more than he was prepared for?

When the door opened and he saw a woman who must be Ruby's mother, his foreboding flared to life.

He should have remembered her mother would be here. He felt as though he was intruding where he didn't belong. He wasn't who either of these people thought.

"Mr. Jones?"

"Damon. You're Ruby's mother?" he said.

"Yes. I'm Bette. Come on in."

He entered their home. It wasn't a large house. It was older, probably built in the fifties. Stairs led up to a covered porch, and now he stood in a small entry off the living room. Wood floors throughout, ahead was the dining room and to his left double French doors led to a sitting room with a bookshelf.

Damon followed Bette through a wide archway into the dining room. That opened to a remodeled kitchen with wooden stools before an island. The house was small but charming, which suited Ruby.

She turned from chopping a tomato and said with a smile, "Hi."

She was so beautiful. "Hi."

"I see you met my mother," she said.

"Yes."

Bette had left the kitchen.

"Would you like anything to drink?" Ruby asked.

Damon looked around for Maya and didn't see her. "What are you having?" he pointed to her glass of dark liquid.

"Iced tea."

"I'll have a glass of that." He stepped into the kitchen. "I'll get it."

"Glasses are up in there." She gestured with her knife to a cabinet. "Pitcher of tea is in the fridge."

He got a glass and put some ice in it from the dispenser on the refrigerator door. Then he poured himself some tea.

Hearing the sound of Maya bounding down the stairs and feet pattering on the floor, Damon turned in time to see her enter the dining room and kitchen. Tall for a five-year-old, she was slender and would surely grow into a beauty like her mother. It made him wonder what his own children would look like. What would Maya look like had he been her father? He hadn't thought much about starting a family, but seeing Ruby's daughter seemed to light something in him, possibilities. Curly brown hair up in a high ponytail that swayed as she moved, her adorable light brown eyes found him. She stopped short, looking suddenly shy. She went to her mother as Bette appeared around the wall. Maya peered around the back of her mother at Damon, who found the whole display utterly charming.

"She was full of energy today," Bette said. "Until now."

"She's always wary when she meets new people." Ruby signed, *It's okay. He's a friend*, then put the bowl of salad in the refrigerator.

Damon knew a little sign language. He hadn't told Ruby that yet.

"I had to ask her to put her toys away. She's hungry and looking forward to ribs," Bette said.

"She'll eat anything."

Maya signed, *Can I have a soda?*

"Sure," Ruby said, signing at the same time, but Damon caught on that Maya could read lips. Ruby took out a soda and gave Maya the can. Then she crouched and signed, *This is my friend Damon.*

Maya looked up at him and signed, *Hello.*

He signed, *Nice to meet you.*

Ruby stood. "You know sign language?"

Seeing her pleasantly surprised look, he said, "Enough to get by."

"Why did you learn?" she asked.

"That's impressive," Bette said. "Ruby's never met a man who can sign."

Ruby sent her a warning look, as though her mother had just given her nod of approval for her to have Damon as her new boyfriend.

"I knew someone who was deaf, a long time ago," he said, hoping she wouldn't ask further. He had learned because he found it useful when he encountered deaf people in his line of work as a DEA agent, whether they be criminals or witnesses.

"A friend?" she asked.

"Yes," he said, again hating that he had to lie.

"Are you still in touch with him? Or her?"

"Him. And no, we drifted apart." The man had been a witness. Not being able to communicate with him had cost him too much time. That's why he had learned sign. "I also happen to have an interest in languages." That was true. "I speak Spanish and a few other languages."

"Wow. Impressive," Ruby said.

Her mother raised her eyebrows and smiled at Ruby.

"So you do have aspirations in life," Ruby said, teasing.

What are asps? Maya signed.

Damon chuckled with Ruby and Bette.

Ruby signed, *Aspirations. They're like wishes.*

I wish I had a daddy, Maya signed to the room at large.

The innocence in her quick glance at Damon cut through him. He had no illusions over what the young girl must have gone through when her father kept her from seeing her mother. Not to mention the line of work he did. The bad people he associated with. A child that age would not have the mental capacity to know it was wrong. She had probably been confused. To her, her father loved her, and she had likely worshiped him. The parent–child relationship was all unconditional until the kids reached an age where they became aware of their individuality. Maya also loved her mother and must have missed her intensely. But being just five, she had no defenses. She hadn't understood the awfulness of being taken from her mother, and now she had no father. Damon wished she had never gone through this. But of course, when she grew up she would realize.

Damon signed, *I'm sure your mother will meet someone nice someday.*

Are you nice?

I like to think so.

Her sweet eyes studied him a while. *Do you like my mommy?*

Yes, I do. He looked up at Ruby with a grin.

"Come on, Maya." Ruby sent Damon a flirtatiously warning look and then took her daughter to the table, where she had a coloring book.

After grappling with guilt over what could be construed as using a five-year-old to get information, Damon grilled the ribs. The activity and the festiveness of it helped take his mind off the true purpose of his presence here. He caught Ruby eyeing him every once in a while, as though reading his mood. Did she know he had tried to get information about Maya's father, or did she wonder how he felt about being involved with a woman who had a child? He suspected it was a little of both. Clearly the subject of her ex was totally and completely off-limits, but why was she so adamant about it? Was she embarrassed? Scared, for sure, and Damon didn't blame her. Mercer and his gang of criminals were dangerous people.

"She's a cute kid," Damon said as he helped her prepare the back patio table.

"I like her just a little," Ruby said with a smile.

Bette had gone inside to get the salad and Maya.

When everything was ready and Maya plopped down on a chair at the table, Damon sat across from her, leaving the chairs beside her for Ruby and Bette. Seeing she had brought her coloring book, Damon leaned forward a bit.

What did you draw? he signed.

Maya signed back, *A horse.*

Damon looked at the black horse and noticed how Maya had stayed inside all the lines. *That's very good. You could be an artist someday.*

Maya smiled big. *My mommy was an artist when she was a kid.*

"Wow." Damon turned to her. "Why did you give it up?"

"It was just something I did growing up. A hobby. I guess you just get busy as an adult." She turned to her daughter. "And then you have children of your own."

Ruby ran her forefinger down Maya's tiny nose, and the girl looked at her mother with love in her eyes.

Damon envied the bond they must have, one that must have grown stronger after being separated for so long. He wanted to know that kind of feeling and to be a part of a family. He had always known he would start a family some day but had never made any concrete plans. Meeting the right woman was the most important element, and he had not met anyone who had made him start to think seriously about that.

Until now, maybe. He looked at Ruby, who caught his gaze.

Ruby blinked as though sensing the somberness of his thoughts. The moment warmed, and Damon had to turn away. Bette saw them and had that approving glint in her eyes.

Unabashedly biting into a rib, Maya watched Damon as she messed up her face and fingers with barbecue sauce.

Damon dug in right along with her, deliberately getting sauce on his face and hands. That made Maya laugh. She bit into the rib again, smearing more sauce. Damon chuckled. The kid was absolutely adorable. What impressed him the most was her deafness didn't seem to deter her at all. At such a young age, her future dawned before her.

"Your daughter is quite intelligent," he said to Ruby.

Ruby beamed with the compliment. "She is. She learns fast. She is going to be a smart girl. She's already smart."

He imagined people who were deaf had to adapt,

be more alert than most. “It’s nice to see a kid adjust so quickly to being deaf,” he said.

“We don’t think of it as a disability, and I work hard at guiding her to keep thinking that way.”

“You must be such a good mom,” he said, meaning every word. “There are moms, and then there are exceptional moms. I think you are one of the latter.”

“She is a great mom,” Bette said. “She learned from the best.”

Ruby smiled at her mother, while Maya spooned some baked beans and shoved them into her mouth, giggling and watching Damon. She must have caught at least some of what he and her mother talked about. He played along, taking a huge bite of beans.

Beans make you fart, she signed.

Ruby put her hand on Maya’s arm. Maya looked at her, and Ruby shook her head. Then Ruby signed, *Manners.*

Maya calmed and resumed eating without fooling around. When she looked at Damon, he winked, for which he was rewarded a cute and secretive smile.

The warm and loving connection he felt just then made him check himself. He didn’t want to lead these two remarkable people into a false reality, but at the same time this felt so personal and…right. What a tragedy that he should meet this nice family and begin to have thoughts of joining them when there was no possible way that could ever happen. When Ruby found out who he really was, she would not forgive him. He would never see any of them again. Best not to get too attached. Maybe that was easier said than done, especially now, after Maya had wormed her way into his heart just by meeting him.

He saw that Ruby had caught the exchange, and she smiled in a way that told him without a doubt how much she liked the way he got along with her daughter. Oh boy, was he ever going to be in trouble.

Chapter 3

Two men sat at the bar drinking the beers Damon had served them. As he worked, Damon could not stop thinking about Ruby and Maya. Bette, too. She would probably make a great mother-in-law. Maya was a special kid. And Ruby…

She was beautiful inside and out. She raised Maya with loving discipline. Damon couldn't stop his feelings from intensifying. He wanted things he had never wanted this much before. He wanted to be with Ruby. He wanted to be a part of Maya's life. This all seemed so absurd, since he had only spent one evening with Maya. Maybe it had more to do with Ruby and the strong attraction he had for her. He had to stop that. He had a job to do. The sooner he wrapped up the undercover case, the less damage he'd do to everyone, himself included.

Frustrated and troubled over the way Ruby refused to talk about Mercer, however, Damon wondered if he should just listen to his gut and ask his boss if he could be removed from the case. It wasn't the first time he'd had this thought. After meeting Maya and seeing how much it meant to Ruby, he contemplated it more seriously. He could quit the bar and tell Ruby everything. Maybe he'd have a chance at earning her forgiveness by withdrawing from the case. Then he could explore their relationship for real. He hadn't seen her in a few days and had had plenty of time to think things over.

The only problem was Ted Reyes had been killed by Mercer's gang, and Damon had personal reasons for going after them. Ted had been a close friend and colleague. He had had a confidential informant, and the two of them had been caught together. It had been assumed that the informant had been discovered by Mercer's other associates and followed. Both of them had been killed, and the shooter had gotten away. Damon hadn't been there but wished he had been, even though there had been no reason for him to be. He had been freshly assigned to this undercover case. He couldn't give up now. He had to bring down the one who'd murdered Ted and the criminals who had ordered the hits.

Damon wiped down the bar after a customer had left, glancing over at a table of three men having beer late in the afternoon. They were Mercer's men, and they had been watching Damon. Word had spread that he was interested in making extra money. The owner of the Foxhole tolerated them and maybe even supported their cause. Damon hadn't witnessed him taking kickbacks, but he had good rapport with most of the members.

The three over there frequented the pub the most. After Kid was killed, Damon had overheard them talking about a man named Santiago. Just that. Santiago. He didn't go by any last name. Apparently he had taken over control of the syndicate. They all called themselves the Nightcrawlers. Worms as far as Damon was concerned. A bunch of reprobates.

Damon suspected Orlando Braxton was the one who'd killed Ted. Six feet tall, longish dark hair, he had brown eyes with a sort of dead stare, never showing any kind emotion. He must be a mean one. Also at the table was Curtis Morgan and Sonny Cooper. They seemed to follow Orlando. After some surveillance, Damon learned those three were Santiago's top men and likely the ones who carried out orders to kill and who oversaw drug deals. They were the men Damon had been targeting to win their trust. He hadn't gotten very far with that, which only added to his inclination to ask to be removed from the case and pursue Ruby.

Just then, he saw Orlando look over at him again and then stand, say something to his pals and start walking toward him. Really? Orlando was going to come over and talk to him? Maybe his luck was about to change.

Orlando approached the bar and took a seat on a stool in front of Damon.

"What can I get you?" Damon asked.

"Beer."

Damon went about pouring him a mug.

"Thomas tells me you do a little business on the side," Orlando said.

Thomas was the owner of Foxhole. "I do. I hear you do, too."

"Maybe."

"Maybe we can help each other," Damon said.

"My boss wants to talk to you," Orlando said. "He's on his way right now. When he arranges for a meeting here, it's expected that the meeting takes place."

Damon understood that all too well. The front door opened, and a man entered. Damon recognized him as someone who came in infrequently but had conversed with some group members and others he didn't know. He only came here for meetings. Damon figured that out just now.

"Ah. Here he is now," Orlando said.

"All right."

"He'll come to the bar. Make sure it's vacated of other customers." Orlando glanced over at the one remaining drinker.

"Of course," Damon said.

Orlando walked away, intercepting Santiago and speaking briefly to him. Damon went to the lone customer.

"Your drinks are on me tonight. Go find a table."

The man looked at him for a few seconds, then glanced toward the door and the table where the other gang member sat. Without a word, he raised his glass of booze to Damon in thanks and walked away.

Damon had learned much of Santiago's operation over the last several months. He began by befriending the members who made up the lower hierarchy of the organization. The people who moved drugs or guns. The people who sold them on the streets. Many of them came to Chicago for meetings. Some operated outside the United States.

The international runners diverted legally purchased weapons from debarred countries. They bribed government officials to move them through those countries without licensing. Government workers didn't make much money, so cash payments were common. They also targeted government stockpiling facilities. The US runners did the same, but it was a lot tougher here when it came to stockpiles. Santiago had made deals with corrupt arms manufacturers.

And then there was his drug operation. That was where he really made most of his money. He had people who transported product across the San Ysidro and Laredo ports of entry and, he was sure, by other methods, such as underground or by boat or plane. It was a big operation.

Damon waited as Santiago walked with the confidence of a ruthless killer to the bar. Alone and without backup possible, Damon had to steel himself into his role as a small-time drug dealer looking to make an alliance with the ruling gang in the community.

Santiago was around five eleven and fairly trim in his fifties. His eyes were dark and beady and lacked emotion of any kind. "Damon Jones?" Santiago said.

"Yes."

"I'm Santiago."

"I know who you are."

"Oh?" Santiago sat. "And how do you know me?"

"I've seen you come in, and Orlando told me you were coming to meet me."

Santiago reached into his expensive-looking inner-jacket pocket. Damon concealed his concern and readiness to respond until he saw the man pull out a pack of cigarettes. There was no smoking allowed in the Foxhole, but Damon didn't object as the man took out a lighter and lit one.

After Santiago puffed a billow of smoke and lowered his hand with the cigarette between two fingers, he asked, "What do you know about me?"

Damon bent to retrieve a short glass and put it near Santiago's burning cigarette to serve as an ashtray.

Santiago's eyes met his in shrewd appreciation.

"What can I get you to drink?" Damon asked.

"Your best whiskey, straight."

Damon gave him what he asked for. "Santiago? You have a last name?"

"Just Santiago."

That was all he wanted Damon to know. Or maybe he did really only go by that name. Everyone knew him as Santiago. As a drug dealer, he was likely proud having one name associated with him. With his commanding, almost six-foot-tall good looks, it suited him.

"I've had my eyes on you over the last few months," Santiago said.

"I've noticed." Damon played it cool. Santiago and his trio of watchdogs would know a lie. Damon had planned for this moment, when he could face the leader and convince him he could be trusted—when he couldn't. This could turn out to be a major break in the case.

"Tell me about yourself," Santiago said.

Damon reached into the reserves of background he'd been trained to recite in situations like this. "What do you want to know?"

"Where did you grow up, and how did you end up here, working at the Foxhole?"

Nothing like getting right to the point. Damon found he liked that about the man, despite his degenerate nature. "I grew up in Detroit and moved to Chicago as soon as I graduated high school. My dad left when I was a kid, and my mom worked two jobs." Telling the lies was so much easier when the recipient was a criminal. "I worked as a bartender at a few other places before finding the Foxhole…and Thomas."

"Thomas is a good man."

Of course he would have that kind of opinion about a man who looked the other way when illegal activities were going on. Those activities had cost Ted his life. Damon had had to face Ted's family after he was killed. He had to quell his anger over the injustice.

"*You* found the Foxhole?"

"Yes. I liked its patronage." That should tell Santiago that Damon had searched for the right place of employment to facilitate his side job, fictitious but essential to the case.

"Its patronage." Santiago was testing him.

"You know exactly what I mean."

Puffing on his cigarette and tapping the ashes into the glass, Santiago studied him.

Taking the hint, Damon expanded on his explanation. "I had a gig back in Detroit, but here in Chicago I've noticed the marketing opportunities are limited." He paused. "I don't want to tread where I'm not welcome, but I'm more than a little interested in investing. I don't want to lead. I want to make some extra cash is all, and like I said, I don't want to tread where I'm not welcome." That should be neutral enough to avoid anyone else hearing him and convince Santiago he was for real.

Santiago met his gaze with deadness similar to Orlando's. "I respect that in a man. Orlando has told me you are cautious. I also respect that. You've left subtle messages of your interest in joining my organization… but are you trustworthy?"

"I never said I wanted to join your organization. I just don't want to start a turf war." Damon shrugged with his hands outspread in a peaceful gesture. "It's just me. I like making extra money, that's all."

Santiago didn't respond. Damon knew he might not accept a connection like that, one that was so individual.

"I'm sure you checked me out," Damon said. "You know my background. Aside from that, every business deal comes with some uncertainties. I'll work with you on terms until you know you can trust me."

Santiago smiled. "That, my friend, might be manageable." He drained the entire glass of whiskey and set the glass down. "But for us to engage in business, there is something I need from you."

This was the part Damon disliked about undercover work. When criminals asked him to do distasteful things.

"How much do you know about Ruby Duarte?" Santiago asked.

Damon should have expected something like this—to involve Ruby. "What does she have to do with anything?"

"We know you've been seeing her."

Of course they did. They had eyes on him. Damon had seen them from time to time. He expected that. He had planned for it. But Ruby's safety was paramount to him.

"I have, just recently." Damon intended to plant a seed of doubt in Santiago's mind. "She works down the street at a coffee shop I go to."

Santiago's brow lowered. "You don't know her association with me?"

"With you?" Damon feigned ignorance. "I'm sorry. I don't know what you're talking about. What association?"

Santiago remained silent.

"Are you planning to use her against me? Like a soft spot?"

Santiago chuckled. "That's always a possibility. Everyone has their weakness."

"I just started seeing her. I'd hardly call that a weakness," Damon said.

With a hard, unreadable look that would be threatening to most people, Santiago met his eyes in silence for several seconds. What was going through his mind? For one, Damon made it clear Ruby wasn't his weakness—thereby protecting her—and for another, he had given this gangster the impression he didn't know Ruby very well.

"Do you know Kid Mercer?" Santiago asked at last.

"Not personally, but I know who he is and that he was killed by a cop." He withheld any further knowledge until he could glean what Santiago was after.

"Ruby was his lady," Santiago said.

"Oh. I get it now," Damon said.

"With his death there have been some changes."

Damon nodded. "One would expect that. I've been wondering who took over in his place. It's good to know the man who did. At last."

Santiago smiled again, though not really genuinely. "I have a proposition for you."

"I'm listening."

"You're in a unique position," Santiago said. "If you really want to do business with me, I need you to help me find out what Ruby knows about Kid's activities before he died."

Join the club. That's what Damon had been trying to do from day one. "What exactly do you want to know?"

Santiago glanced around. The bar was vacant, and only two tables were occupied, one with Orlando and his crew, the other with two men engaged in what appeared to be an intent conversation.

"Just what I asked… What does she know about Kid?"

Damon realized he'd have to give this man something. He had to be careful. Anything he revealed could put Ruby's life in danger, and Maya's.

"I have noticed something," Damon said. "I've asked Ruby about her daughter's father, but she's been closemouthed about it—to the extreme."

Santiago nodded. "She knows more than she lets on."

"What do you want me to do?"

"Get her to talk." Santiago leaned back, more relaxed as he must have begun to trust Damon. "Mercer had a stash of guns and ammunition."

What? Damon had to hide his astonishment. He and his team knew nothing of this.

"My organization depended on the revenue from the sale of them," Santiago said.

"I can understand that," Damon said.

"And we need them. Now."

Damon nodded. "You want me to find out where they are, and then we can do business?" Damon asked.

"Yes." Santiago looked satisfied. His dead eyes actually came to life for a brief few seconds.

Damon's mind reeled. This had to be why Ruby was so afraid, why she never talked about Mercer. New resolve came over him. He would fight hard to get her to open up. Not just for the sake of his undercover case, but more so to save her and Maya.

Ruby had another evening to herself. Maya and her mother were asleep, and she enjoyed a cup of tea and a book—or she tried to.

Damon had to work late again, and he'd be at the pub until after two in the morning. They had been seeing each other almost every day. Ruby was afraid to let herself feel what she knew was bursting to be free from her heart. Heck, she probably had already done that.

Ruby had thought a lot about why she was so against talking about Kid. Yes, she was humiliated and felt like a bad mom for her inability to protect the one person who meant absolutely the most to her, but Damon seemed like someone she could lean on. It was the latter that had her so reluctant to trust him. He *seemed* trustworthy…but was he? He was a bartender, but he was clearly capable of more. That's what bothered Ruby the most. Instinct warned her not to let him in too deep. She had that feeling early on, just a few months after he had started coming for coffee. Why was she so attracted to him? He didn't seem to fit his current profession.

Aside from his sexiness, he had intelligence. And an affinity with kids. With her daughter. And her mother. And her… Ruby herself. He was kind and sure of himself.

She had felt similarly about Kid when she had first met him. Kind, charming, good-looking. He had convinced her he had the same long-term goals. Family. Security. Love. He had seemed to have a lot to offer. She had wondered about his profession as a nightclub owner, but his business had a good reputation and was upscale. Her main concern was how much time he would be away from her. And any kids they had. But he had reassured her—convincingly—that he would delegate accordingly so he could have regular hours. Ruby had believed him.

Now here she was, involved with a man who was a bartender—not a nightclub, but still too similar. Kid had been a charming snake. She couldn't say Damon was a snake, but he had charm. The biggest difference between them was Damon wasn't as secretive as Kid. Kid had a scary distance about him. She had learned the magnitude of that too late.

A knock on the door startled her. She checked the time. Just after nine. Alarm sent her into defense mode. Her daughter and mother were asleep in the house. It was late for a visitor.

Carefully and silently she made her way to the door. Peering through the peephole, she saw Damon.

Why was he here at this hour?

She opened the door a crack.

"I'm sorry to have come here so late and unannounced," he said. "I had a weird conversation with someone tonight, and I needed to make sure you were okay."

A weird conversation? "Who?"

"A guy named Santiago."

Ruby didn't know anyone by that name.

"Let me in so we can talk." Damon looked around as though fearful he'd be seen. Ruby didn't want that, so she opened the door.

Her heart now raced with unknown possibilities. The unknown was always the most terrifying.

They went into the living room, where she didn't feel like sitting. She folded her arms and faced him.

He put his hands on his hips and took in her stance, not appearing to like it. "Santiago is part of a drug organization, and he knows you and I are seeing each other."

Her jaw lowered and shock ravaged her. She had never heard that name before. Kid had surrounded himself with people who had nothing to do with the complexities of his business. She had never met the men who worked closest with him. Kid had made sure of that. He had lured her along his deceitful path for as long as he could.

"Who is Santiago?" she asked.

His head angled as though he thought she should know. When she said nothing, he said, "Apparently he took over for Kid Mercer. Your ex."

Her mouth opened, in further shock. Thoughts and questions bombarded her. "Wha…why are you talking to people like that?" Never in million years would she have expected this. Why was this coming out now—with Damon? Was it a coincidence? What were the odds? Now he was connected to Kid's gang? And her?

"I bartend at a place they frequent."

"Down the street?" She had moved, but she hadn't moved far. She had moved far enough away from Kid's nightclub. Just her luck that his gangers took a liking to the very same pub where Damon tended bar.

"He approached me," Damon said.

Damon hadn't known Kid's gang members went to the Foxhole? Was it only after the man named Santiago had contacted him that he had learned Ruby had had a relationship with a drug dealer? Ruby had to gather her aplomb. And failed. This was serious. She thought of Maya and what this could mean for her precious little girl and nearly lost control.

"But…how does he know we're seeing each other? How does he know me?" She heard her own fear in her voice. She began to tremble. This was exactly what she had always dreaded: Kid's men coming after her.

"I don't know, but they don't seem like the type to let things go very easily. I was uncomfortable talking to the man."

Ruby had no doubt about that. She fidgeted with her fingers. What was she going to do? Maya…

"When are you going to tell me about your ex?" Damon asked. "This doesn't seem like a good situation we're in."

"I left Kid as soon as I found out what he was into. He and his friends aren't part of my life anymore." That wasn't exactly how it had gone, but she had planned on leaving him and taking Maya with her. And she couldn't be certain that part of her life was over. Kid still haunted her, even in death.

"What was he into?"

"Drugs." Oh, she so did not want to let that part of her past into her life now. She had worked so hard to get Maya therapy and to move on, to make her and Maya's life better, safer. With the help of January Colton and Detective Sean Stafford, that had seemed like an attainable dream. Now she wasn't so sure. Her fears seemed to be coming true.

"Anything else?" Damon asked.

She looked at him, dazed and confused as to why he'd ask that. Then she grew apprehensive. What else could there be? Did he think she knew more? "Isn't drugs enough?"

Damon studied her a while. Did he doubt her? Why would he care?

Then he stepped toward her, looking apologetic. He opened his arms to her. She didn't resist or try to stop him. She needed comfort. She didn't know who she could trust, but Damon was the one person she felt she could. More than anyone else, anyway.

He gently took her into his arms, his hands rubbing her back. “Don’t worry. I’ll handle him.”

He would handle a drug dealer? “How? He could be extremely dangerous.”

“I’ve dealt with his kind before,” he said.

She leaned back to look him in the eyes. “You have?”

His hesitation set her on alert.

“I’m a bartender,” he said. “I’ve worked in places that attract that sort of people.”

That seemed like an adequate explanation, but Ruby had a feeling he was hiding something. “Why bartending?” She couldn’t shake the feeling he was doing more, that he had more ambitions than that.

After a brief hesitation that raised her suspicion higher, he said, “I was young. I went into the service industry and ended up bartending. It seemed like a good thing at the time.”

He was still young enough to change all that. “Do you see yourself moving on to something else?”

His mouth crooked up on the right side. “Of course. I don’t want to serve drinks the rest of my life.” He chuckled.

His lightness eased her wariness. “What do you dream of doing?”

“Dream? I don’t dream. When I decide to do something, I do it,” he said.

She certainly liked his confidence and believed he meant every word. “What are your choices? What do your aspirations tell you?”

“I’ve thought about law enforcement.”

She moved back a step, surprised by his declaration. "Really?"

"Yeah. I get tired of watching bullies and criminals. Sometimes I wish I could do something," he said.

She smiled, liking him even more now. He did strike her as the upstanding type, the type who would go up against the Kid Mercers of the world.

"I didn't know Kid was a drug dealer until it was too late. He duped me. Don't think for a minute that I don't berate myself for allowing that to happen. But if I hadn't been with him, I wouldn't have Maya."

"Don't be too hard on yourself. Those people are good at lying and cheating their way through life. They don't care about anyone other than themselves and their own personal gains."

Ruby stepped close again, going back into his arms. "Tell me more about you," she said with a tone that spoke her heartfelt wishes. He'd shared some details about himself, but it all seemed…rehearsed. She hadn't realized that until now.

Ruby wanted to know him. She wanted to know everything about him.

When his expression closed, a foreboding certainty came over her that there were things about him he hadn't shared. She began to withdraw, her defenses rising higher. She did not need another bad mistake. Another really, really bad mistake.

"I'm who you see me as," Damon said.

He moved even closer, but Ruby stepped back, too apprehensive of the unknowns about him.

But he drew her to him, hooked an arm behind

her. She found herself pressed against his impressively hard-muscled body. Her hand automatically came up and landed on his chest.

"All you need to know right now is the only thing that matters to me is you, your safety, and Maya's," he said.

All she needed to know?

Before she could rebut, he pressed a commanding kiss on her mouth. Electric sparks spread and tingled. Ruby lost all coherent thought. She only felt Damon, his hands on her, his mouth working magic with hers.

He slid his hand farther around her and pulled her against him. She looped her arms around his shoulders and angled her head to get more of him. He responded by deepening the kiss. The play of tongues made her hotter for him. If this went much further, they'd end up in bed. Or on the floor. Right here.

But then his hands covered the side of her breast. Heat shot to her abdomen. She did what she had been dreaming of doing ever since she'd first seen him. She pressed her hands to his hard stomach and moved up to his chest. She felt his broad shoulders and returned to his chest before treating herself to his back and finally his rear.

He lifted his mouth from hers and met her eyes, his breath mingling with hers and his eyes hot. With her hands still on his rear, she began to feel him grow hard. This was not like her, not after Kid. She did not get bold with men. She'd gone on some dates, but she had not gone this far with anyone since then.

Slowly, he brought his mouth to hers again, this

time not ravaging. He made love to her, soft and thorough. Their lips matched in movement and poignancy.

Ruby slid her hands around to his front and reveling in his fit torso again before placing one hand on his shoulder and sinking the fingers of her other into his hair. He had magnificent hair. Shaggy in the right places.

Turning with her in a half circle, he backed her up against the dining-room wall. Then he pulled up her shirt. So out of her mind with desire, Ruby lifted her arms and away went the shirt. She unbuttoned his shirt and parted it. Then she planted kisses on his chest, running her tongue over his nipples and going lower to his abs.

He unclasped her bra, and it slipped off. She rose up, and he looked at her bareness. His rapt attention thrilled her and turned her on even more. He touched her, and she put her hands on his forearms, feeling the muscles work lightly as he caressed. He lifted her, using the wall as support, and put his mouth over one breast.

Ruby wrapped her legs around his hips and closed her eyes to lovely sensation. She dug her fingers into his hair again.

Kissing his way up her neck to her mouth, he kissed her with more purpose. Hard and driving. Ruby met his verve with her own, reeling with how spectacular she felt.

Damon began to move his erection against her. She was on for him. In the next few moments they *would* be on the floor.

Ruby had to stop. "Damon."

She sounded so breathless.

He withdrew and looked at her. She saw the raging passion in his eyes and knew it mirrored hers. They were combusting on desire for each other.

He had however, gotten her mind off Kid's gang—if only for a few moments. A few glorious, startling and maybe even scary moments. What lay ahead for them now? What wasn't he telling her?

Chapter 4

Ruby was so glad Damon insisted on staying the night. He slept on the couch and had acted as though he had been just as shaken up by the kiss as she. It wasn't so much the kiss, it was the potency of it.

He was already up when she appeared in the kitchen, making what appeared to be pancakes.

"You're going to spoil her rotten," Ruby said.

He chuckled. "I love pancakes."

"Who doesn't love pancakes?"

"My fat cells." He patted his stomach.

He hardly had anything to worry about. She had felt those hard abs when he pressed her against him. The man was definitely fit.

"Is Maya up?" he asked.

"I'm going to let her sleep in. She looked too sweet to wake up."

He smiled. “She is something. Does she miss her dad?”

Ruby knew he was curious about her ex. He must be doubly curious now. She didn’t like talking about her past with Kid, but it was time to tell him. She trusted him enough now.

“I think she misses her father, but somewhere in her little heart she sensed he wasn’t a good man. Kids have a way of looking up to their parents no matter what.”

“I know you were afraid of Maya’s father,” he said. “I knew early on. Your face says a lot, whether you realize it or not.”

“My mother always told me I was a terrible liar.”

“Honorable people are terrible liars,” he said.

Gee, thanks. She sighed, dreading talking about Kid. It soured her stomach and brought back feelings she never wanted to remember or feel again.

“I didn’t know Kid very well when I got pregnant,” she said. “It was an accident…getting pregnant. But Kid was elated. I thought it was the beginning of something wonderful. A family. A man to love.” She grunted derisively. “Boy, did I ever get that wrong.”

“Everybody makes mistakes,” he said.

She looked at him. “Not everyone makes that big of a mistake.”

“What do you mean?”

She averted her head, embarrassed at what she considered extreme stupidity. “After about two years I began to notice things.”

“It’s okay, you don’t have to talk about this. I know it upsets you.”

“No. It’s okay. You and I are close enough now,

and I want you to know." She reached out and put her hand on his arm.

He appeared touched by what she said. Then he blinked a few times. "That means a lot to me, Ruby."

She smiled a little and then dropped her hand to rub her forehead. Then she continued. "Kid was so secretive about his business, which I always found odd. He owned a nightclub. What was so sensitive about that?" Folding her arms, she looked around the kitchen, not liking the memories flooding her. "His livelihood should have been my first warning. He was rarely home, never at night. Every time I asked him about his work, he got defensive. Then one night I overheard him talking to someone in his home office. They were discussing a drug deal."

This would reveal just how debauched her choice in a man had been. And what had led to her failure to protect Maya. She had felt like a terrible mother.

"Kid Mercer was a drug dealer," she said. "A high-ranking one. He was also an arms dealer and became very powerful. I was appalled. My only thought was of Maya. I had to get her out of there." Ruby lowered her head, on the verge of a surge of tears.

"You don't have to do this, Ruby," Damon repeated.

He sounded so caring, as though he cared more about her than knowing her history.

She shook her head. Looking up at him, she said, "This feels right. Telling you. It's hard, but it's right."

She met his eyes, which appeared as traumatized as she felt. She fell for him even more in that moment. He was such a good and decent man. So different from Kid's lying and violent ways.

"Kid caught me trying to leave with Maya," she said. "He had his men take Maya from me and forced me to leave. He kept my own daughter from me for almost three years."

"That's terrible. What kind of person would do that?"

"An unscrupulous one. One who has no empathy. A criminal," she said bitterly. "I got her back after police shot and killed him in an altercation. He was going to be arrested and resisted. Mightily." She wiped her cheek as a tear slipped past her defenses, and she lowered her head.

Damon tipped her chin up. "I'm sorry you had to go through that," he said. "You don't have to be afraid anymore, Ruby. I won't let anyone harm you."

He pressed his lips to hers in what seemed to be a comforting kiss but ignited into something completely different. Looking into his kind and honest hazel-green eyes, she recalled their kiss last night and had an instant desire to share another.

"I'm not afraid when I'm with you. You make me feel safe," she murmured. "Like this is a good thing."

"I feel the same."

"You've had a bad relationship before?" she asked.

He nodded ruefully. "I was engaged once. I found out she was sleeping with another man. It's your typical heartbreak story, except she really did a number on me. I don't like thinking about her, much less talking about her."

"Have you been with anyone else since then?" she asked.

"Not like that. I've dated since then, but not with

anyone that would last…and not for a long time." He met her eyes as he finished the last of his sentence. The importance of mutual respect clearly meant the same to each of them.

A wave of strong attraction engulfed Ruby. He was such a man. A real man. "Well, maybe knowing each other will get us both past our bad decisions." She felt so good saying that.

"I'd like that," he said in a raspy voice.

With nothing further to say on the matter, Ruby let the chemistry between them warm up before moving closer and touching his lips. She kissed him lightly but lingered a while to let him know how invested she was in him right now. She slid her hand up his chest, seeing the flare of heat in his eyes. He held her around her back, not too tight, a loose and gentle embrace. Patient.

At last the kiss ended, and she could breathe again. Ruby looked up at him, dazed and giddy with new romance. She hadn't expected the kiss to be so strong last night. This morning it was tender and full of promise.

Hearing Maya approach, Ruby moved back from Damon to see her rubbing her lovely light brown eyes, her medium-brown hair all messy from sleep.

Mommy, I'm hungry.

"Well, it just so happens that Damon made us pancakes." Ruby signed as she spoke.

Maya brightened in an instant. *Cool!*

Damon put their plates on the table, and they all sat like a real family. Ruby had never been happier in her entire life. Seeing Maya watch Damon, she knew he would make a great father for her. Could her life finally be headed to a good place?

* * *

Damon didn't feel right about continuing to see Ruby. A few days had passed, and he missed her way too much. He could tell she genuinely liked and trusted him. She wouldn't have confided in him about Kid otherwise. He had met her daughter, someone more precious to her than anyone else on the planet. He was honored that she had opened her heart to him, but his duplicity would not go unpunished.

By now, she was probably wondering why he hadn't called or come by. She was probably also afraid. Maybe feeling alone. Another arrow for his heart. What she didn't know was he was keeping an eye on her. Well, not him but another agent. Tonight he sat with a nature program playing at a low volume and a calming cup of tea. One of those herbal numbers. It wasn't working.

His phone rang, and he saw it was his brother Nash, a year older than him. His spirits lifted. An architect with a Chicago firm, Nash had found success and purpose in his life. He had been close to their mother and had taken her death hard. But Nicole had been there for both of them. She had been a great mom. Damon doubted Nash would have had the drive to become an architect without her loving guidance.

"Hey, bro," Damon said.

"Checking in on you, danger-seeker," Nash said.

Although he teased, Damon knew his brother meant his high-octane job as a DEA agent. "How are you doing?"

"Fine. Working a lot. You?"

"Fine. Working a lot."

Nash laughed, and so did Damon. This small talk wasn't like them.

"Dad called," Nash said. "Surprised me until I realized he must have an agenda."

"Grandfather's will?" Damon asked.

"He didn't say it directly, but he played nice with me, like he was trying to smooth over our relationship to prepare me for whatever he wants. It disgusted me."

Growing up, Nash had had difficulty with their father's apathetic parenting. There had been a lot of yelling and neglect. He was all right now, but he had no soft spot for Erik Colton.

"We can always block his calls," Damon said.

"What? And miss the entertainment?"

Damon chuckled. "That's a healthy way of looking at it."

"Uncle Rick is the only father I ever had," Nash said.

"I feel the same." A memory struck him. "You remember the first time you called Nicole *Mom*?" Nash hadn't had an easy time adjusting to their mother's death.

"I was in high school."

"Took you long enough."

Nash laughed a little. "She's an amazing person."

"You seeing anyone?" Damon asked.

"No. The good ones are already taken. You're probably closer than me. Women dig agents."

"No, they don't. Not the good ones." Ruby didn't like him because he was an agent. She didn't even know he was one.

"Yeah," Nash said soberly. "But hey, that's not why I

called. Our cheating grandfather's real family is having a postholiday party, and we're invited."

"What?" It was August.

"Yeah. They want to get to know us better. If you weren't so deep undercover you would know."

It was true. He hadn't been to his real home in months. "They want to get to know us?"

"Yes. And I think it's a noble gesture. None of us kids have been on board with Grandmother's unquenchable vengeance for being the rejected mistress."

"Very eloquently put, brother."

Nash chuckled.

"Are you going to make it?" Nash asked.

Doing so could ruin his cover. "I don't know. I hadn't really thought about it."

"You should be there. We have a huge family now. And our cousins seem to genuinely want to know us."

Damon had picked up on that, too. He didn't want to miss a family event like that. He wanted to get to know the people he had not known existed until recently.

"I'm working," Damon said.

"That's all you do is work. I'm not asking for days or weeks. Just one night. Come on. Let's go together. You, me and Aaron."

Aaron their half brother, who was every bit a full brother to Damon and Nash. "I'll try."

"No. You commit right now. You're going."

Damon did want to go. The party was this Saturday. He had that night off. Besides, he needed some time away from Mercer's men and Ruby. And Maya. That whole family-feeling he had with them.

"All right. You and Aaron pick me up, brother." He'd

be careful not to be seen leaving or coming home. It wasn't his usual practice to mix his personal life with work—especially when he worked undercover, but he needed a break. And he wanted to know more about the cousins he had only recently learned existed.

Damon stood in Farrah Colton's Tuscan-inspired mansion, feeling a little awkward among the cousins who were basically strangers. He also worried he'd taken an undue risk coming here while working an undercover case. He had been careful not to be followed, but there was always that chance he'd be discovered.

What Damon knew about his new cousins was limited, but they were the progeny of Damon's grandfather Dean Colton and his wife Anna. Damon's siblings were the children of Dean Colton and his mistress, Carin Pedersen. Damon found it ironic that Dean's wandering lust had been passed down to his sons—all four of them, two sets of twins. What were the odds? Dean must have had a massively dominant twin gene in him. Ernest and Alfred's mother was Anna, which made Damon's cousins legitimate. Damon's uncle Axel and his father Erik were the illegitimate sons of Dean's mistress, Carin.

Damon, his brother Nash and their half brother Aaron had only recently been introduced to their legitimate cousins. They had always known their grandmother had had an affair with a prominent Colton, but that side of the family had never been part of their lives. Damon, like his brothers, had not thought much on it—until their conniving, bitter grandmother had come up with a scandal to use her sons as a tool to take an inheritance that didn't belong to them.

"Do you think this is as weird as I do?"

Damon glanced over at Nash and held back a sudden urge to laugh. "Weird. Yes. I was just thinking there are a lot of twins in our family."

Nash did laugh but kept it low. "We're in the house of one twin."

Farrah Colton's twin was Fallon. Farrah had married Alfred, and Fallon had married Ernest. Both husbands had been murdered. From what Damon understood, it had been a random killing. A couple of nineteen-year-olds knocked off some people on a spree. It was freakish. Ernest and Alfred were leaving work late and were shot. Senseless. He had been so busy, he hadn't had time to delve into the details. He had been more interested in the people, his extended family. Family had always been important to him. But his head spun with all the drama on top of discovering he had such a huge family.

"They're doing very well." Nash glanced around the elegant furnishings.

"Do all of them live like this?" Damon asked.

"I don't know. I assume so." The inheritance had been quite large.

Damon glanced around at the throng of people. There were many from the community in attendance, but Coltons made up the majority. He felt like he had been dropped into the middle of a *Succession* episode. It was so not his thing. But he never backed down in the name of doing what was right, and what was right here was not taking money that didn't belong to him or anyone in his immediate family.

"Do you know who our cousins are?" Damon asked.

Aaron appeared to his left just then. "I just got all the introductions." He looked across the room. "Farrah's three daughters are over there. Simone, Tatum and January." He searched the room and stopped his gaze on a man standing near a bar with an attendant standing behind it. "That man over there is Heath, the oldest of Fallon's kids."

Seeing them, Heath walked over. "You must be Damon and Nash." He looked from Nash to Damon.

"I'm Damon."

Heath reached out a hand, and they shook. Heath had dark blond hair and shadowy stubble. He studied Damon directly with dark blue eyes.

"Good to meet you." He turned to Nash and shook his hand. "I already met Aaron, here."

"Heath is president of Colton Connections," Aaron said. "They do inventions."

Damon had heard that. "Your family is very successful."

"So is yours. Aaron told me he owns some gyms and Nash here is an architect. You're a DEA agent. That's impressive."

Damon thought it was generous of him to say such nice things when his father and uncle were trying to clean them out of their inheritance.

"Why don't I take you around to meet everyone?" Heath said to both Nash and Damon. Then he turned to Aaron. "You're welcome to join us if you like."

"I'm good. I'll go talk to Myles and Lila. They just arrived."

Damon saw his cousins on their side of the railroad track enter the room. "We'll catch up with them later." He was glad to see them. They were all very close, and their stepdad was like a father to him and his brothers, had been ever since their mother died.

Heath led the way toward an athletically built blonde and another fit body, a male with dark brown hair.

"Hey, Heath," the woman said, giving him a hug. "Are you commandeering the room like you do at work?"

Heath chuckled. "Just being social. This is Damon and Nash Colton." He turned to the aforementioned men. "This is my sparky sister Carly and my brother Jones. Carly is a nurse at the University of Chicago hospital. Jones owns the Lone Wolf Brewery. We were all so excited to have an opportunity to get to know our new cousins."

"We were," Carly said.

"None of us knew anything about you," Jones said, reaching out a hand to shake Damon's and Nash's hands.

Carly didn't do the same, but her welcoming smile said all that needed to be said. Again, Damon was overwhelmed with how friendly these people were. Could it be they had loving parents who cared more about their well-being than money?

"You are all being very gracious given the circumstances," Damon said.

"From what I've seen, you aren't the ones on the offensive," Heath said. "It's your fathers, Erik and Axel."

"The one to truly blame would be our grandmother," Nash said. "We're kind of the bastard sons of a bastard son."

Nothing like putting it bluntly…

"I'd rather think of it like we're all family here," Carly said, this time without a smile. She meant it.

For the first time since arriving, Damon felt relaxed. Like he and his brothers belonged.

"Thank you for saying that," Damon said.

"You better be careful with this one. He's a DEA agent."

"A real badass," Jones said.

"I'm not a badass. I just think doing what's right and protecting people is important," he said.

"He was raised by someone who taught him what was wrong," Nash said. "As was I."

The three others laughed good-naturedly.

"We figured you had that attitude, and we can't say we're glad, because it's your dad and grandmother," Heath said. "They are family. Just know that we have felt similar conflict in our family."

"You had a good father," Nash said.

"Yes, but not so much for a grandfather," Heath said. "Our dads were definitely good. Innovative and inspirational."

Damon didn't say he wished he could say the same. Now wasn't the time or place to have that kind of discussion. Maybe later as he felt out the rest of the cousins.

Heath's fiancée came over to join them, and Nash got into a discussion with the two of them. Damon excused himself and headed over to where Farrah's three daughters stood talking and laughing, holding champagne flutes.

All three smiled as he approached.

He introduced himself.

"This is Simone and Tatum, and I'm January."

"Nice to meet you. I might have trouble remembering who is who after this."

The three laughed, and he smiled. "I do know you're all Farrah's children." And they were all attractive just like their mother. Simone had chin-length brown hair and blue eyes, Tatum had long, gorgeous blond hair and blue eyes like her sister, and January had long wavy blond hair and green eyes. She looked like a model, despite being around six or seven months pregnant.

"We've heard so much about all of you," January said. "It was so shocking to realize we had so many cousins."

"It was shocking for us, too," Damon said. "I was flattered to be invited here tonight." They certainly didn't have to do that. It was a nice gesture.

"We all wanted to get to know you."

Despite the circumstances? "We wanted the same." He glanced around at all the other Coltons. "You all must be like siblings rather than cousins, being born from twins."

"Yes." January's eyes brightened. "We are all very close."

"I'm close with my brothers. We also have a really awesome uncle. Rick Yates. He was like a father to us."

"Oh, that's great," January said. "Well, it's all of our wish to get to know you all and have a family relationship if that's possible."

"After meeting you, I think it is," Damon said. "And on that note, I wanted to tell you in person how sorry I was to hear about your father and his brother."

"Thank you," January said. "It's been very difficult."

"I get the impression your father and his brother were much better men than my father and uncle," he said.

"Well, it is true our father and uncle were respected men. We don't want you to feel bad about how your father and uncle behave. One could argue it isn't their fault, given the way they were raised," Tatum said.

"Yes, and our grandfather isn't exempt from blame here," Simone said.

He had cheated on his wife, yes. And his sons hadn't. Not the story on Damon's side of the family.

"My brothers and I have talked, and we intend to try and stop Carin from railroading you. We all know it isn't fair, and none of us want or need the money. We are all financially comfortable. We aren't those types of men." There: he had said what he'd planned to say.

All three women bestowed him with adoring, appreciative smiles.

"Why aren't you married yet?" January asked.

He thought of Ruby and wondered why she had popped into his head at that moment with the mention of marriage. He pushed it out of his head. He did not wish to go there yet.

"I am. Soon to be divorced."

"Oh, well…whoever ends up with you is one lucky lady," Simone said.

"I could say the same about you, except it would be one lucky man."

"Try three. They're all taken."

Damon turned to see a man with light brown hair approach. He leaned in and kissed January.

"This is my fiancé, Sean Stafford," January said, beaming as Sean put his arm around her. "He's a detective for Chicago PD."

She also sounded proud. Damon didn't see that kind of love very often, but it radiated off this couple.

"I take it you are married?" Damon asked the other two women.

Tatum smiled. "Not yet." She pointed a few feet away where a group of men stood talking. "The one in the middle is my boyfriend. He also works at Chicago PD, but he's in Narcotics. The slightly taller one is Simone's. He's an FBI agent. So you see, you'll fit right in as a DEA agent."

Nice. Lots of law-enforcement types in the family.

"What do you ladies do for a living?" They didn't strike him as the kind of women who would settle for letting a man take care of them. They were too stong and confident.

"Simone is a professor of psychology, and Tatum is a chef who owns True."

"I've heard of that restaurant," Damon said. It was a good one.

"I'm just a lowly social worker," January said.

"She's being too humble," Sean said. "January cares a great deal about the children she helps."

The more Damon learned about his new cousins, the more he realized what good people they were. He considered it his lucky day and was glad he had taken the risk in coming here tonight.

Seeing his brothers together with their cousins from the so-called other side, Damon said, "Will you excuse me?"

"Of course," January said. "I'm sure we'll be seeing more of each other from here on out."

"I'd like that." He left feeling good about his future and gaining an extended family. More than ever that seemed important. Tantamount, actually. He wore a closemouthed smile that could burst into a full-out, white-toothed happy thing.

Lila and Myles were together now. Not talking to others at the gathering. Damon had a backward thought that his instincts as an agent, working undercover cases, had allowed him to see they were as out of sorts as him. Even with his absolute fascination with his other cousins, he was still in covert mode. That could be good or bad. He voted for the good, since that would give him the best leverage with Ruby once she discovered his true identity. And she would. That was inevitable.

He closed off those thoughts. He needed to gather around the family right now.

Lila hugged him, and Myles next.

"How are you doing?" Lila asked.

"Good, actually. What do you think of all this?"

Nash and Aaron walked up, standing next to Lila. It felt like a wrong-side-of-the-tracks communion.

Damon looked out through the throng of people in the rich environment. He knew his brothers and cousins did the same, picking out their privileged cousins.

Damon had no ill feelings. No instincts that told him these people were bad—like his father and uncle.

"I think we should fight the suit," Aaron said.

Damon looked at him, and Aaron met his gaze.

"And I mean *really* fight it."

"With them," Nash said, giving a nod to the groups of cousins targeted by Carin.

Damon chuckled, feeling good about all of this and connected in ways he had never been before. He only wished Ruby could be here with him.

With that thought, he was reminded of his duplicity and how impossible it would be for them to be together if she ever found out who he really was.

He inwardly corrected himself.

When she found out who he really was. His only hope was controlling how and when she did.

Chapter 5

Ruby was on cloud nine. No. Ten, eleven or twelve. Whatever number could be assigned to how astronomically good she felt. She walked up the beautifully lighted path toward Farrah Colton's front entry, two white pillars supporting a gabled roof. The Tuscan-style house was a mansion to Ruby. She had never been here before, nor had she met Farrah. January was her daughter, who had invited Ruby to this epic, if not iconic, postholiday party.

January had cousins she never knew, and they'd all be here tonight, but the Coltons had invited many others. The main objective, as January had told her, was to get to know her long-lost cousins. This was a party to break the ultimate ice. Christmas in August!

Ruby was in the perfect mood for a celebration. Her

spirits couldn't be higher, and Damon was responsible. He was a good and strong and honorable man. Nothing like Kid Mercer. Ugh. That was such a horrible time in her life. Damon had turned that all around in the months she had known him.

And Maya adored him.

Her heart soared with joy over that. Her mother–daughter bond was finally intact, and she believed she had found a man who could fill the final void. A real father for her daughter.

And a real husband for her...

She stopped those thoughts. She had to be cautious. A good marriage to a handsome and loving man seemed like a fairy tale. Could it be she'd have that with Damon?

Walking toward the front entry, Ruby felt like a princess in her best dress, which would pale in comparison to probably most of the other women at the party tonight. A white flowing sleeveless, it was a good replica of something expensive. Her heels were soundless against the crafted concrete pathway, thanks to good soles.

A butler let her in. She entered the party, a little late in getting there. Maya hadn't wanted her to go, and she had to do some comforting first. Her mother had gotten her set up with a cartoon, and she would be going to bed soon.

Arriving by herself was disconcerting. She didn't recognize anyone. She only knew January and Sean. Searching for them, she didn't see them through the crowd of people. As she expected, most were dressed elegantly. There was a lot of money here tonight. She had never been to a party like this. Kid had thrown some elaborate ones, but they had all been odd, at least to her. That was the word she had for those events. *Odd.* The people had a nice facade, but the vibes had always been…dangerous. From their body language, which had always been on the tough side to the way they dressed, some in leather, some with body piercings and tattoos on their faces, and nearly everywhere else visible, and men with bold jewelry. She had always been uncomfortable, even apprehensive.

Sean was the kind of detective who truly cared about not only the victims of crime but the families affected by it. He had done her a big favor when he had gone after Kid and tried to arrest him. Kid had been shot and killed in the altercation. Ruby wasn't upset at all. With Kid gone, she could have her daughter back. Both Sean and January had developed a close relationship with Maya. They cared about her a great deal and would have adopted her until they learned the girl had a mother who was alive. They had not only helped her get her daughter back, they had given a heavenly hand. They had gently reunited Maya with her mother.

She spotted them standing in the huge and opulently beautiful living room. Although richly decorated, it had a warm feel.

Ruby smiled big, genuinely glad to see January. She leaned in for a hug. "It's so good to see you."

They were the same height. January was blonde, and Ruby was dark-haired. Ruby felt as though January could be something of a sister to her. And an aunt to Maya. Ruby had already made her and Sean her daughter's godparents.

"You look fantastic!" January exclaimed, moving back with Ruby's hands in hers and looking her over.

"Not nearly as fantastic as you," Ruby said. January wore a knee-length sparkly cocktail dress that didn't hide her pregnancy. Ruby looked down at her round tummy. "How are the twins?"

January put her hand on her stomach. "They're active. And I mean it. You look great."

"Thank you."

"How is Maya?" January asked. "I miss her so much."

Ruby would have to arrange to bring Maya around her more often. She had been so focused on her daughter's well-being that she thought of little else.

"She's doing really well," Ruby said. "Thanks to you and Sean." She looked at Sean to include him.

"I just did my job," Sean said.

He had saved Maya from a dangerous man. Ruby's ex.

"No, really," Ruby said. "The therapy you helped me set up did wonders for Maya. I feel like she's a normal child now. She chatters more. Plays more. Laughs more. And she isn't having so many bad dreams."

"That's great, Ruby. She's a sweet little girl."

Ruby couldn't agree more. "I'm almost grateful she was so young when Kid took her from me. I hope she doesn't remember much of it, if anything, especially the terrible things she must have seen." Things no child should have to witness, the biggest one being the murders in the warehouse where police had found her hiding.

"Oh," January said, her hand going to her heart, indicating how touched she was.

"We'll plan a barbecue or something so you can spend some time with her." January knew sign language and had been instrumental in bringing Maya out of a bad situation and helping Sean solve his case.

"We won't miss it," Sean said.

"Not for anything," January added. "How is school going? Are you managing all right? Is there anything you need? I feel like it's been so long since I've talked with you."

"School is going great. My mother watches Maya while I work and attend classes. She is really getting the hang of being a grandmother. And Maya just loves her. It feels like I am part of a family. A real family. At last." Ruby thought of Damon and hoped the beaming happiness she felt just then didn't show too much on her face.

January studied her face with a knowing smile. "Are you seeing anyone? That's a look that says you are."

Drat. She never was good at hiding her feelings. She wasn't sure she wanted to talk about Damon. They were still so new at their intimate relationship. Well, maybe not *that* new, after nearly having sex the other day and being acquainted for several months.

"Yes. I am," Ruby admitted.

January's mouth opened with a soft gasp. "Who is he?"

"This sounds like it's going to be girl talk," Sean said. He kissed January on her cheek.

She looked into his eyes, and Ruby could feel their love in that exchange.

"I'll catch up with you later," Sean said.

"Okay." January kissed his lips, and Sean lingered a bit before moving away.

After he left, January faced Ruby. "Okay, I want details. Tell me everything about him. How did you meet? What's his name? Is he cute?"

Ruby laughed lightly. "He's a bartender at a pub down the street from where I work. He's been coming in for coffee for months, and we've gradually gotten to know each other. And I wouldn't call him cute. He's extremely handsome, though."

"Wooo, look at you. It's all over your face that you really like this guy," January said.

"Yes. Our schedules are very different, but we've managed to see a lot of each other."

"So he kept coming for coffee, huh?"

"Yes." Ruby remembered the first time he came in. She was struck by how tall and handsome he was, in a rugged sort of way. When he ordered his coffee, she had melted at the sound of his deep voice. "He stared at me but didn't ask me my name. He came in a few times a week, and we'd have small talk, until eventually he asked my name and told me his. He would always have funny stories to tell about what happened at the bar the night before. They were much better than mine about the goings-on at Mostly Books."

"He sounds nice. Takes it slow?"

"He took it very slow, which I needed. It's almost as if he knew."

"Some men can be intuitive that way."

Ruby couldn't help smiling. "He is the exact opposite of Kid." At least she hoped. She still harbored some hesitancy there.

"So you're dating now?"

"Yes." Ruby beamed some more. "We've been on quite a few dates, and he's met Maya. He knows sign language. Can you believe that? And Maya likes him. He's good with her."

"Ruby, that is wonderful. You deserve a good man."

Just then Sean returned. That hadn't taken him long. But he had someone in tow. A somewhat older woman. Short curly dark brown hair, she was almost as tall as Ruby and January and wore a long flowing white dress.

"Sorry to interrupt, ladies, but there's someone I want Ruby to meet. Farrah, this is Ruby, Maya's mother," Sean said. "Ruby Duarte, this is January's mother, Farrah."

"Ah." January had told her the party would be held at her mother's house. "You have a very beautiful home."

"Why, thank you." Farrah sounded as genuine as her daughter January.

"My mother owns an interior-design company with my aunt, Fallon," January said. "They're twins. I don't know if I ever told you that."

Ruby didn't recall if she had. "That seems like a really creative profession." She could have cringed at how unintelligent that comment sounded.

"January told me so much about you and Maya," Farrah said. "I'm so happy things are going well for you now."

"If it weren't for January and Sean, I don't know that I'd be where I am."

Farrah turned adoring eyes to January, obviously proud. Then she looked back at Ruby. "I don't mean to brag, but I did raise three incredible daughters."

Ruby heard the sincerity and didn't take it as bragging. "Thank you for inviting me to this party. I'm truly honored."

"We wouldn't have it any other way," January said.

As with any grand party where there were so many prominent people, Farrah was whisked away by a man Ruby didn't pretend to know, much less his importance. There must be many here who were influential in town.

"Something to drink, Ruby?" Sean asked.

"I'll find my way to the bar." She didn't plan on drinking alcohol. She had a daughter to go home to.

Sean and January took up talk with another couple she again didn't recognize. She began to feel out of place, like a single person who intruded on the interactions of two couples who obviously were familiar with each other.

"Excuse me," Ruby said.

January turned her head and smiled. "I'll catch up with you."

Her friendliness always made her feel so welcome. When she first learned where her daughter was, she had been so worried she'd never get the little girl back. Social workers were involved. She had feared her association with Kid would be her lifelong ruin. But to her great relief, January had given Maya a safe refuge, and Ruby had been reunited with the one thing that meant the absolute most to her.

Ruby looked around. Maybe there was a lone person somewhere she could strike up a conversation with. She was in a roomful of people who were way out of her class. She had expected this party to be extravagant, but nothing could have prepared her for not only the number of invitees but also the wealthy elegance. January and Sean were so humble. Ruby bet most of the others in this throng weren't.

She meandered her way to a bar set up just for this party. "Ginger ale, please."

The black-coated bartender gave a nod and got her a glass full of ice and the soda, plopping in a straw and a festive umbrella.

Ruby turned and moved to a tall cocktail table, taking out the umbrella and covertly putting it there. Sipping from the straw, she scanned the crowd of chattering rich people amid classical music playing at an appropriate volume. This was so not her scene. She liked classical music, but she wouldn't play it at home. She was more of a pop and country girl.

She decided to entertain herself by just watching everyone. She'd stay long enough to be polite and then leave.

Taking another sip, her roaming gaze caught sight of someone familiar.

What?

She knew that face. That was…

Damon.

What was he doing here? A bartender from the Foxhole…*here*? It didn't fit.

Confusion gave way to a shock wave. His presence here meant something was wrong. He didn't belong here. She could argue neither did she, but what were the odds he'd be at a Colton party?

Her heart slammed. Her breathing became restricted. She could not process what this meant. She didn't want to. She didn't want to face it. Not after all the magic.

A cocktail waitress approached, holding a tray. "Can I get you anything?"

Ruby pointed to Damon. "Do you know who that man is? The one with dark blond hair and a short beard."

"That's Damon Colton. Like all the other Colton men, everyone else notices him, too."

Ruby shook herself into coherency. "I-I'm sorry. Did you say *Colton*?"

"Yes. I'm surprised you didn't know. Everyone knows who all the Coltons are. Especially the men." The waitress winked. "Are you doing all right on that drink?"

"Y-yes." She felt her whole world tilt and whirl as though in a horrible cesspool, just as it had the day Kid had taken Maya from her. The taste of betrayal was familiar.

"Are you all right?" the waitress asked.

"Yes. I-I'm fine."

"You look like you just saw a ghost."

Ruby didn't respond, and the waitress walked away with a concerned look.

Just then Damon turned after laughing at whatever he and two other men were talking about. His gaze caught hers, and he froze. His white-toothed smile faded. They stared at each other for a timeless moment. Then he put his beer down on a table and started toward her.

Ruby's first desire was to get away, to get him out of her life. He had obviously been lying to her for months. But she needed some kind of explanation in order to put this behind her.

As he strode toward her, his handsome manliness speared her with loss. All that she knew about him was a lie. Her heart longed to feel good about her attraction to him, but it was only physical now. He wasn't who he had said he was.

"Ruby?" He stopped before her. "What are you doing here?"

Her shocking pain gave way to indignant affront. "Excuse me? What are *you* doing here, Damon *Colton*?"

His wary, questioning look smoothed into resignation. "I wanted to tell you."

"Tell me what? That you've been lying to me all this time?"

"I work for the DEA. I'm an agent and my case is to investigate Kid Mercer's gang. I've been working undercover. Blowing it could cost me my life."

Ruby nodded cynically and looked away, not really seeing all the people enjoying themselves while her world crashed and burned. Undercover agent. Kid's gang. Bartender working down the street from Mostly Books…

It had all been planned. He had gotten the bartending job at the Foxhole because that's where Kid's gang hung out. Ruby hadn't known that, but Damon must have. He must have also known she worked down the street.

She returned her gaze to him, numbness beginning to come over her. "I let you meet my daughter."

Damon blinked slowly, his guilt showing. "Ruby, I never meant to hurt you. I wanted to tell you so many times."

"But first you needed me to tell you what I knew about Kid," she said.

"That was initially the plan, but after I got to know you—"

"Stop." She put her hand up. "Don't try to tell me it was real."

"It was. Not at first, but—"

"You infiltrated my life as part of your investigation. You got the job at the Foxhole, and you came into Mostly Books to worm your way closer to me."

Damon looked defenseless now. He said nothing. What could he say to the truth?

"You asked me out on a date. You *dated* me!" And they had very nearly had sex. Thankfully, it hadn't gone that far.

"That part wasn't a lie," he said.

"Oh, so you didn't ask me out to further your investigation?" she snapped.

Damon sighed hard. "Ruby, I did have to carry out my investigation."

"And asking me out on that first date was part of it." She wanted to force him to admit it.

He sighed again, this time shorter and in two frustrated breaths. "All right. Yes, but—"

"That's all I need to know." Ruby marched away, searching for January. She had to keep it together long enough to get out of here.

"Ruby, wait." Damon took her arm and stopped her.

Pain seeped back into her as she met his magnetizing hazel-green eyes.

"I asked you out on a date to try and get information about Kid, but the date itself wasn't part of that. You and I were not part of that. You have to believe me. I know you felt it, too."

Oh, that drove a knife through her and ground out her heart. She yanked her arm away.

"You should never have let it go as far as it did while you were making me believe you were someone *else*!"

He had that defenseless look again. He couldn't argue that point. He never would be able to.

Ruby turned and went to January, whose smile faded when she saw her. She walked to Ruby, and the two stood face-to-face.

"Ruby, what's wrong?"

"That man I told you about?" Ruby turned her head to where Damon still stood, watching. "He's the bartender at the Foxhole. He's a DEA agent, and he's been working undercover to investigate Kid Mercer's gang."

Despite her best effort, tears burned her eyes.

January looked from Ruby to Damon and then back to Ruby. "I didn't know, Ruby. I mean, I knew he worked for the DEA, but I didn't know anything about his investigation. Neither did Sean, or he would have told me."

"It's not your fault. Damon lied to me."

"And hurt you. I can see that. Would you like to go somewhere private to talk?"

Ruby shook her head. "I just need to go home. I wanted to thank you again for inviting me. I'll be in touch so you can see Maya again."

"Maybe you shouldn't drive. I can arrange for someone to drive you."

"No. I'll be all right." Ruby smiled woefully. "If I survived Kid, I can survive anyone."

"I'll call and check on you in a few days," January said.

"Okay." Ruby appreciated her friendship, especially now.

Walking toward the front door, Ruby glanced at Damon, who watched her go. Each step away from him sealed her fate. No more Damon. No more dreams of a happy family. Ruby just wasn't destined to have that in her life. She had Maya, and that was enough. She'd keep telling herself that, anyway.

All Damon could do was watch Ruby walk out of his life. So many things went through his head. Only pain and regret went through his heart. There was nothing he could say to her that would make her understand. Not right now. She needed time. But that meant she'd be alone. In danger. He'd worry about her every waking moment.

He caught sight of January approaching. *Here we go*, he thought. Another reprimand. He wished both women knew he didn't need it. He had already reprimanded himself more than once.

"What happened?" January asked. "Ruby was really upset."

"I know. I didn't mean for her to find out this way," he said. "I couldn't tell her."

"She really liked you, Damon. She told me about you."

She had? "What did she say?"

"She said you were the opposite of Kid."

"I am definitely the opposite of Kid." He supposed he should be glad she at least thought that about him. Maybe not anymore, though.

"Sean and I knew you were working the Mercer case, but we didn't know you were undercover," January said.

"That's the whole point of working undercover. You don't tell anyone." At least his sense of humor was still intact.

"I didn't think Ruby was involved, but now, in retrospect, I should have. She was with Mercer. She had a child with him. The DEA would want to find out what she knows about him."

"Would you have warned her if you had?" Damon asked.

January seemed to ponder that a moment, averting her gaze and passing a glance around the lavish room. "I'm sorry to say, but yes, I think I would have. You probably broke her heart."

Damon didn't doubt he'd hurt her. He regretted that to his core. He had dreaded the day she'd find out the truth. He just hadn't expected it to come this soon.

He looked around at all the Coltons and felt removed from it all. Gone was the celebratory mood he'd felt before. He was still shocked over the unlikelihood of Ruby knowing anyone here—or the unlikelihood he had perceived. He hadn't even considered the possibility.

"She beamed when she was talking about you," January said. "She thought she'd met a really great guy."

She thought right, but getting her to believe that now might be impossible. "I didn't pretend about that. I did need information from her, but her and I? That was real."

"Well, did you get the information you needed?" she asked, seeming satisfied by his declaration but doubtful as to Ruby's happy ending.

He grunted. "No. I don't think she knows anything."

January put her hand on his upper arm. "I hope you can find a way to win her back. She deserves someone good."

She still thought he was good? "Thanks for the vote of confidence. I'm going to need it."

"That you are." January smiled and left him standing there contemplating the road ahead. The curvy, uphill road. What was he going to do? He couldn't leave her to her own defenses, not with Santiago on the prowl.

Ruby stepped into a quiet house. It was just after nine. Her mother must have gone to bed. Ruby was relieved. She needed to be alone. After kicking off her shoes and setting her purse aside, she went to Maya's bedroom door. She always liked the door open. A seashell night-light kept the boogeyman away.

Walking to the bed, she sat beside a soundly sleeping Maya and lightly brushed some hair off her face. Leaning over, she kissed her soft cheek. And then just watched her sweet, peaceful slumber.

At least Ruby would always have her.

Going downstairs, she went into the kitchen and made a cup of chamomile tea. Once that was ready, she took it to the living room and sat on the sofa with her legs curled under her. Holding the steaming concoction that normally would relax her, she knew it would not tonight.

She left the television off, lest she wake her mother. Left alone with her thoughts, she was overwhelmed with how duped she'd been by Damon. He was certainly good at his job. Did he only work undercover? If so, his whole outlook on life would be so warped. He worked with criminals like Kid. Pretending to be just like them. Well, if a man pretended for too long, he became just like them, didn't he?

Ruby had been so cautious. She had no regrets over the due diligence in screening a man who wasn't good for her. She hadn't done anything except protect herself and her daughter. But what was a girl to do when the man she met presented himself as someone full of integrity, when in fact he was just a good actor? A role player with a staunch resolve to solve a case—no matter the toll it took on the innocent.

Who was he?

A Colton. That's pretty much all she knew about him at this point.

January was a Colton. She was a good person. Was Damon? Despite his lies?

It did not matter. Ruby had been through hell with

Kid. She had her daughter back. Dreams of a husband who would be father to her daughter and make them a family were gone. She had been foolish to think she could have that. She had been foolish to trust anyone with Maya's future. More than that, she had been selfish.

Maya had been through enough. Ruby had almost sacrificed her again. That was unforgivable. Ruby would not—not ever—trust anyone ever again.

Someone knocked on her door.

Alarm chased through her. Was it Damon? She sat where she was for several seconds, waiting for a second knock.

It never came.

It was late for someone to knock on her door. Apprehension brought out the mama bear in her. She'd be damned if anyone would ever take her daughter from her again.

Getting up, she quietly made her way to the door. Sliding the peephole cover aside, she peered through it and saw no one outside.

She went to the front window, staying to the side of the frame. As she slowly leaned over, she parted the blinds just enough to see. Nothing stirred outside. Outdoor lights illuminated the street. Neighbors always had their houselights on. Ruby saw nothing move.

She looked toward the entry. From here, she couldn't see if anyone stood at the door.

Taking a deep breath, she went to the front door and peered through the peephole once more.

No one.

Maybe it was a late package delivery. She unlocked the door. Opened it a fraction. Saw no one was there. She looked down and saw a note under a small rock, flapping in the breeze.

Searching around again, she opened the door enough for her to crouch and retrieve the note, quickly bringing it in and closing and locking the door.

She lifted the note.

We are watching you.

Ruby's hand trembled with the obvious threat. What perplexed her was she already suspected she was being watched by Kid's cohorts. Why did they feel the need to make this kind of announcement? She didn't understand. If they thought she knew something valuable that only she would be able to provide them now that Kid was dead, why send this anonymous and quite late message?

They must be aware she knew Kid was involved in drugs. Did they assume she knew more about his business dealings? If so, her life and her daughter's life were both in greater danger than she'd originally projected.

What was she going to do?

Stay up all night, for one. Try not to obsess over Damon's betrayal for another…

Chapter 6

Ruby finding out his true identity couldn't have happened at a worse time. Santiago's not-so-veiled threat that he had to find out what she knew put her in great danger. Alone, with a five-year-old, she couldn't know the risk. Not the way he did. That was one thing. The other… What were the odds she actually *knew* a member of his family? He was still poleaxed over that. He couldn't have predicted that if he had tried. He hadn't seen that coming, not by a long shot. When he had first spotted her standing there at the party, he couldn't believe his eyes. At first he thought she just looked like Ruby, dressed to the nines and stunningly gorgeous. But, oh no. It was Ruby. Her icy eyes had bored into him.

Disbelief had given way to shock, and that had

given way to dread. He didn't blame her for not wanting anything to do with him. He would have reacted the same way. He had reacted the same way when his ex, Laurel, had slept with another man. She had told him it wasn't the first time she had kept two or three men on the side. Her lame excuse had been that she needed lots of sex. When he told her he was capable of satisfying her, she said she liked variety—as in more than one on the side. It was a living fantasy for her. Having sex with one man knowing she had just been with two others and in the next day or two she'd be with a third turned her on.

Well, that very well might be, but it wasn't fair to the person with whom she pledged fidelity. Damon had gone straight to the doctor to check for diseases. Why had she even agreed to marry him? She had even tried to convince him they could have a healthy, albeit open, marriage.

He'd told her to get lost.

Then he had begun a long road to recovering from his gross misjudgment of character. He was trained to read people, to predict their behavior and act accordingly. She had duped him completely and totally. Granted, he had been young and new at his job, but he should have recognized the signs.

That was why he couldn't blame Ruby. When he had watched Ruby leave, he knew he had to give her time. He gave her two days before trying to call. That was this morning. She didn't answer. If he ever earned her respect and trust back, it would be a miracle.

Damon was sitting on Nash's back patio, sipping beer with the outdoor television playing a baseball game. He wasn't much into watching baseball, but the sound was cheerful. It had been a couple of days since the party. The atmosphere, the game or Nash's manicured backyard and stone patio didn't lift his mood. As an architect, his brother had bought this craftsman bungalow and fixed it up. The place had loads of charm.

"What's got you all in the dumps?" Nash asked, returning from inside to take the chair beside him, separated by a small table with a bucket of iced beer. There was a round patio table with an umbrella next to them.

Damon glanced over, surprised his mood showed. He normally didn't expose himself like that.

"My case," he said simply.

Nash observed him as only a man who knew his brother would. "I haven't seen you this way since Laurel showed her true colors. Who is she this time?"

The sound of someone opening the patio door spared Damon from responding. But only for a moment.

Rick Yates stepped out onto the patio, bringing with him his trademark air of upbeat positivity. Five ten with a full head of gray hair and a goatee, he said, "Nash said you were going to be here, so I had to come by. We haven't seen much of you in the last several months."

"He's been working a case," Nash said.

"Is it over? Did you get some more bad guys?" Rick asked, moving a patio chair closer to them and sitting.

"Not yet," Damon said. "You know I can't talk about my undercover cases."

"Yeah, but you can talk about the woman you met on it," Nash said.

"You met someone?" Rick asked. "Is she pretty?"

"He doesn't want to talk about it," Nash said, teasing.

"Oh, come on. You're with family. What's wrong, Damon?" Rick asked.

Sixty years young, Rick Yates was more of a father than his own had been to him. Erik's twin Axel had married Vita, who divorced him and married Rick, and it had been all about family ever since. Rick loved big gatherings and often had Sunday barbecues.

"Nothing," Damon said, annoyed.

"Oh, now, you know your uncle won't fall for that. Come on. Out with it."

"It has something to do with his case, but he has the look of a man besieged by thoughts of a woman," Nash said, his handsome face grinning.

Damon loved his uncle, but some things were best left alone. He didn't say anything.

Nash leaned toward the bucket of beer and took one out, cracking open the top.

"How's the plant nursery going?" Damon asked, an obvious ploy to steer the topic away from him. He owned Yates's Yards plant nursery with Damon's aunt Vita. They sold garden plants and flowers and other landscaping items. The business sat on six acres, with the nursery in the front and a big house behind that. Damon loved all the fruit trees.

"Nice try. You know it's going good. Now, out with it."

Uncle Rick would not let it go now. Damon was resigned to his fate and said, “Ruby Duarte was involved with a criminal whose organization I’m investigating. She found out I’m with the DEA.”

“Ahh,” Nash said. “So you and she are an item now, huh?”

“Were. She doesn’t want anything to do with me.”

Rick sobered. Damon was glad he wouldn’t tease. That was Rick. He cared deeply about his family and what happened in their lives.

“I’m happy to hear you found someone who makes you want to keep her, Damon. The ones who make you feel like that are worth every effort. Look at me and Vita.”

He and Vita did have an awesome relationship, and it was obvious Rick loved her.

“Well, I’m afraid I blew it with her,” Damon said. “I know what it feels like to be betrayed by someone I thought I knew. That’s how she’s feeling right now.”

“That doesn’t mean you should give up,” Rick said.

Damon looked out across Nash’s big backyard. A hawk circled above, searching out some poor, unsuspecting rodent. Ruby wouldn’t talk to him. He had tried calling today, and she hadn’t picked up.

“What’s her story?” Rick asked.

“She’s beautiful inside and out and has a five-year-old daughter,” Damon said, knowing he was only scratching the surface of what made Ruby Ruby.

“Walking into a new family can be good. It was for me. Look how you both turned out.”

Rick had a way of making family gatherings festive and full of warmth. The bigger the party the better, as long as it was all family. Vita's daughter was Lila, and her son was Myles. Lila managed an art gallery, and Myles was married and had a son. He was a lawyer.

"I told her my name was Damon Jones and I was a bartender," Damon said. "Then she showed up at Farrah's for the party. Apparently she knows January." Damon stewed over his bad luck once again.

"She was bound to find out one way or another," Nash said. "She'd have been upset no matter what."

"How does she know January?" Rick asked.

Damon could see by his expression he thought that was extraordinary, just as Damon had.

"I don't know." That was another reason why he wanted to talk to her.

"Well, the sooner you get to patching things up with her, the sooner she'll start to trust you again," Rick said. "Trust is everything."

"Thanks for reminding me," Damon said.

"Tell us more about her. What does she do?" Rick asked. "Does she have family here in Chicago?"

"She's in nursing school. Her mother lives with her, and she has a brother and sister in Wisconsin. That's where she's from." There was a lot more he could say about her, that she was kind and warm and stunningly beautiful, but he didn't say it.

"Call her. If she doesn't answer, then go to her house," Rick said.

Damon took out his phone and called Ruby. As with all the other times, she didn't answer. He held up the phone. "No answer."

"Then, go to her house," Rick said. "I've waited

a long time for you to find a woman you can love. I won't let you stand by and let her slip through your fingers. Go get her!"

Damon took Rick's direct advice and drove to Ruby's house the next day. He told himself it was mostly out of concern for her safety, but his heart said it was much more than that. He missed her to the point of pain. His heart hurt. The depth of his feelings for her caught him off guard. He wasn't prepared for this. He had never felt this way before. He needed Ruby. He needed her in his life. That frightened him, but he could not stay away.

He rang the bell. As he expected, she didn't answer. He knew she was home because her green Toyota Prius was in the driveway. After a third ring, he began pounding on the door.

"Ruby?" he said loudly. "I know you're in there."

Nothing.

He pounded again, longer this time. "I'm not leaving until we talk!"

After a few seconds, the door opened, and Ruby's mother appeared. "She's being stubborn."

"I get that about her. It's one of the things I like about her."

Bette smiled. "I've been trying to get her to listen to your side, just so you know."

Damon grinned. "It's good to know I have someone in my corner."

"Well, I wouldn't say I'm in your corner, but I did get a strong impression that you were a good man.

You're a DEA agent. You are no criminal. My Ruby deserves someone on the right side of the law."

"That I am, ma'am."

Bette opened the door wider and stepped aside. "She's in the kitchen."

"Don't do it, Mother," Damon heard Ruby snarl.

"He's on his way."

Damon walked to the kitchen, finding Ruby with her hand on the kitchen island, looking displeased.

"We need to talk," he said.

"I've said all I need to say, and I don't want to hear anything more from you," she answered.

Damon walked up to her, deliberately standing close, hoping to melt some of her stubborn resolve. She tipped her chin up and eyed him defiantly.

This was not going to be easy. "I'm sorry I had to lie to you."

"I don't even know you," she said.

"I told you. Not everything was a lie. I told you about my family. I just didn't tell you their names. And my name is Damon. Just not Damon Jones."

"No, it's *Colton*."

"All right. I did go to college. I got a degree in criminal justice."

"Oh, gee. Lucky me."

Damon angled his head. "I also told you about Laurel."

"Your ex-fiancée?"

"Yes."

She contemplated him a moment. "Damon, I can't just flip a switch and start trusting you again. I fell for Kid not knowing who he really was, and I almost did again with you. I completely believed everything you said. How am I supposed to know you're a good person? You were acting the whole time."

"I am a good person. I'm a DEA agent. I told you the truth about my fascination with superheroes. What I didn't tell you is the reason why. My father, Erik Colton, is not a good person. He only cares about himself and material possessions and money. I grew up envying superheroes. And my Uncle Rick was more of a father to us than my own." These were things he'd wanted to tell her before now but couldn't. "You see, my dad is a twin, and his brother is my uncle, but my aunt divorced him and married Uncle Rick. My brother Nash and I are the sons from our father's affair with our mother, who did die when we were kids—another thing I didn't lie about. Nicole was married to Erik and took me and Nash in after Mom died. She raised us as her own."

"January told me some of the story about your family," Ruby said, sounding more relaxed. "It's big."

"Yes, and getting bigger now that we have met our new cousins," he said.

He met her eyes and could feel her struggle with forgiving him. He didn't expect her to immediately. He just had to make sure she was safe.

Just then, Maya came bounding into the kitchen. She had on blue jeans and a T-shirt that said *Her Royal Fiveness.* And her brown ponytail swayed.

Hi, Damon, she signed, eyes bright with vitality and happiness.

"Hi, Maya." He signed the greeting as well.

I'm glad you're back.

Damon signed that he wasn't back. He just needed to talk to her mother.

Ruby touched her daughter's head, getting her to look up at her. *Go watch your cartoon.*

Maya turned to Damon. *Come back.*

I'll try, but it's up to your mom.

Maya tipped her head up to see her mother. *I want him to come back.*

Ruby pointed toward the living room and signed, *Go watch your cartoon.*

Maya did as she was told. Damon was touched by her kinship toward him. He had never had a child look up to him like that.

Alone with Ruby, Damon had a point to make, and he hoped to lower Ruby's guard enough to let him protect her.

"Are we finished?" Ruby asked.

"Not quite. I need to talk to you about my case," he said.

Ruby turned to a cutting board where she had been in the process of making a salad. "I can't help you with that."

"I need to be sure you're all right," he said.

Ruby looked out the patio door. What was she looking for? Mercer's men? Did she fear they'd come after her? She should.

"I am all right."

"Ruby…" How could he convince her she shouldn't be alone right now?

"You still haven't solved your case. How will I know you aren't still trying to use me?"

"I never intended to *use* you, Ruby. You have information about Mercer that I need."

"Do I?"

He went to stand beside her. "Truthfully, I wondered about that. I didn't think you knew anything that would help me make arrests. Then I began to have feelings for you, and I didn't like playing a role, deceiving you. That's why I considered being pulled from the case."

"But you didn't."

"No, because this is bigger than me. It isn't only about arresting a bunch of murderers and criminals. I lost a friend and colleague because of them. He had a family and was a good man. He didn't deserve to be snuffed out like that."

Damon saw Ruby recognize his passion. He was a man of justice. He upheld right and hated wrong. He actively defended and fought them respectively.

"What happened to him?" she asked.

"He was shot when he met with a confidential informant. The informant was killed, too."

Her mouth frowned in sympathy. "I'm sorry about your friend. Truly, I am. I can see you're doing what you feel you have to do, and for good reason. I can't say I wouldn't do the same."

While that all sounded encouraging, she had a tone that led up to a wordless *but*. He was doing what he had to do and that had included lying to her.

"Ruby, most of what I told you was the truth," he said.

She nodded. "Maybe. But when you were lying, I couldn't tell at all. I still can't tell the difference between you when you lied and when you didn't. All I know for sure is you are a really, really good liar."

"I have to be. If I'm not, then I'm a dead man," he said. Didn't she understand that?

"I thought we were headed for something meaningful."

"Maybe we are." He wasn't ready to commit to that yet.

"Maybe."

Despite the fact it would probably be the nail in a coffin that represented the end of them as a couple, he could not mislead her. "Yes, maybe."

She seemed all the more disappointed. "I thought things were going well between us."

"They were," he said.

"No, I mean well enough to start thinking about the future."

What had she thought? That he would propose? Already? It had been seven months since they had first met, but just a couple of weeks since they'd begun dating, but Damon was not a man who dove into anything serious with a woman, not anymore.

"I had more than one reason for taking it slow with you," he said. "The case, and my engagement to a woman I should never have trusted."

Ruby scoffed at that. "Well, then you have an idea how I feel right now."

He was forced to acknowledge that. "I know what it's like to be betrayed. My relationship with Laurel was different than this, though. I thought she was someone other than who she really was, and she deliberately misled me."

"Like you did with me," Ruby said. "Sounds exactly the same to me."

"She lied about her past and about her feelings for me. I never lied to you about either of those things."

She studied him a while. "So you don't have any plans to be with a woman long-term?"

"Plans? No. I'm open to the possibility, but it will have to be right. I have to be sure. And it's too soon for us. Surely you can understand that. You didn't want to rush into anything, either."

"No, but it's been a long time."

Was she arguing they should become a committed couple?

Suddenly, she closed her eyes and waved her hands as though negating what she just said. "I'm getting off track." She looked at him with new resolve. "It's good you don't want anything lasting with me. I don't want anything lasting with you, either. I'll never be able to trust you, which I'm sure you can relate to. I bet you'd never trust Laurel again."

No, he wouldn't. "That's different. She was sleeping with someone else. Who wants to marry someone who has no principles when it comes to that?"

"Who wants to be with someone who made them believe they were a bartender when in fact they were an undercover agent?" she said.

Damon sighed. He'd get nowhere with her today. His first concern was her and Maya's safety.

"I think you should come and stay with me. You and Maya shouldn't be alone," he said. She might not trust him or like him much right now, but she had to see she was in danger.

"I'm not alone. My mother is here."

"You could be putting her in danger."

That gave her pause, he saw. She averted her eyes, brow lowering in consternation. She would be defenseless by herself. Her mother would be no help.

"She might be in more danger if she's here alone. What if they hold her hostage?"

"Is there somewhere she can go until this blows over?"

Ruby looked out the patio door again, then through the side kitchen window, where she must have a partial view of the street.

"Has something happened?" he asked. "You seem nervous."

"I've been nervous ever since Kid was killed," she said.

He watched her for a bit. She fidgeted with her hands, and fear joined the consternation in her eyes. He had seen her like this before, but now she seemed more concerned. "You would tell me if something happened, right?"

She put down the knife and turned to face him. "You mean like you told me things when I didn't know who you were?"

Frustrated, Damon sighed. "Ruby, come on. I'm worried about you."

Ruby met his eyes, and he saw a flicker of wavering stubbornness.

"Don't let what's going on between us stop you from being safe," he said.

"I can be safe without you. If I need help, I'll call 911."

"If you get the chance."

She lowered her head and folded her arms. He decided not to push her more. He was going into the bar tomorrow. He'd get a sense of how impatient Santiago was getting.

"At least call me if you need someone to be with you and Maya. And send your mother away."

"I'll send my mother away."

Damon heard doubt in her tone. She was considering staying with him. That was good. She had twenty-four hours to come to her senses. He'd lure Maya and put Ruby over his shoulder and carry her out of this house if he had to.

He moved closer to her and put his fingers under her chin, tipping her head just a bit. Enough to touch her lips with his. Just a brief reminder of how good they were together—and also of his determination.

When he finished, he held her gaze with his. "Most of it was real, Ruby."

"Was it?" Her gaze flitted between his eyes. "Or are you just very good at your job?"

She thought he was manipulating her right now.

"Let me prove it to you," he said.

"How can you do that? Propose marriage to me?"

Was she challenging him? Baiting him to see what he would say?

"I don't think we're there yet, Ruby." He still had trust issues from the last time he had proposed marriage.

"No, you aren't there yet, Damon, because you were never there. You never felt the same as me. You were doing your *job*."

"That isn't fair. I told you about Laurel, how she cheated on me. I never saw it coming. You aren't the only one who made a mistake with someone. You can't have that all to yourself. Other people have been hurt and betrayed, too."

"So are you saying you have no plans to get married and have kids?" she asked.

"No, that is not what I'm saying. I think I will eventually. I just haven't planned on when."

"You would know by now if you felt strong enough about me to at least consider it," she said.

"Have you?" he asked. He truly wanted to know. "Do you feel strong enough about me to consider it?"

She averted her face, and he had his answer. She wasn't any more certain than he. She had trust issues the same as him. Different circumstances, but their experiences had done the same kind of damage.

"Let's just agree to get along for now, all right?" he said. "I need to keep you safe, Ruby."

She looked at him for several seconds. "I'll think about staying with you until your investigation is over."

He nodded. That would have to be enough for now. "Thank you. I'll stop by tomorrow afternoon, then."

"All right."

He backed away from her. "Keep all your windows and doors locked."

"I will."

Damon turned to go, hoping it was safe to leave her alone. He didn't think so, but he knew she did need some more time. He'd drive by a couple of times tonight just to be sure. He didn't like leaving her like this. He also didn't like what their conversation today had dredged up. He thought he was long over Laurel's betrayal. Turns out it was still fresh. For the first time since the weeks after he'd discovered her treachery, he wasn't sure he'd ever be ready again for marriage.

Chapter 7

Ruby struggled with Damon's suggestion to stay with him. For a very real reason, she wondered if she should not hesitate to accept his offer. He was right. She was in danger. Her daughter was in danger. But she had no recourse. Local police couldn't help her in the short-term. She had no friends well versed in dangerous people. She only had Damon's expertise. The note said Kid's men were watching her. It hadn't said they'd take any action. It hadn't said they'd harm her if she didn't deliver whatever they demanded.

She hadn't slept much last night. She kept getting up and looking out windows. Her mother had agreed to go stay with her brother and had packed and left this morning, her parting words still echoing.

"Go stay with Damon, Ruby."

She had called work and said she wouldn't be in the rest of the week. She also wasn't going to class. Her professors had agreed to let her make up the coursework.

Maya sat at the dining-room table coloring, and Ruby was in the living room watching the news, trying to calm her nerves.

The doorbell rang, and she all but leaped off the chair. Going to the door, shock and fear zapped her. She recognized Sonny Cooper. He had been one of Kid's men. Average height with dirty-blond hair, his blue eyes were creepy. Fear palpitated through her.

"I know you're in there, Ruby. I need to talk to you," Sonny said through the door.

"What do you want?" she asked, picking up her cell phone from the console by the door. Should she call 911?

"Let me in," Sonny said.

Ruby remembered seeing all of Kid's men carrying guns. She tried to calm her nerves. Her heart raced.

"I can't. My daughter is here."

"All the more reason to let me in. If you don't, I'm going to break down this door."

She'd like to see him try. It was a metal door. But he could break a window and still get in. Or go around to the back and break in there. She didn't want to cause Maya any trauma.

"If you do that, I'll call the cops." She held up her phone and tapped in 911 without connecting the call.

"They won't get here in time to help you. Let me in. All I want to do is talk. I'm not going to hurt you or your daughter."

Said the snake to the cute and cuddly chipmunk.

Ruby glanced at Maya, who still colored as though an evil man were not on the other side of the door.

"I'll come outside." Ruby opened the door a crack and glanced up and down the street. A neighbor was walking their dog, and cars passed.

She stepped outside and closed the door behind her.

Sonny observed her. "You're looking good."

What a sicko. "What do you want?" she demanded harshly. Her mama-bear instinct kicked in. She would do anything to protect her daughter.

"I want what my boss wants, and that is to find out where Kid stashed a significant amount of valuable guns and ammunition."

"I don't know anything about that. Kid didn't share his work with me."

That didn't seem to please Sonny much. "You know, I always liked you, Ruby. You were always nice to me."

"I try to be nice to everyone." No matter how despicable they happened to be. Being nice sometimes was a life-preserving strategy, but a man like Sonny wouldn't understand that.

"See, I think you do know something. And if you don't, then that adorable little girl in there probably does, since she was with Kid up until he went and got himself capped."

"Maya would have told me or her therapist, and she hasn't. She doesn't know anything. She's only five years old. Keep her out of this."

Sonny leaned close, his ice-blue eyes threatening. "This is a courtesy visit, Ruby. If you won't tell me where the weapons are, then tell that boyfriend of yours. Either way, I need to know."

"Is Damon working with you now?" she asked.

"In a manner of speaking." Sonny straightened.

What did he mean? Was he worming his way into Kid's organization? That made sense, since it was his investigation.

Sonny leaned close again. "You only get this one courtesy visit."

"Was that note a courtesy, too?" She probably should keep her tone polite rather than sarcastic, but she couldn't help it. She despised everything this man stood for. And a fighter rose up to protect her daughter.

"Yes, it was. Santiago asked me to first send you the note and then pay you a visit. The next time we cross paths, it won't be good for you. Give Santiago what he wants."

"I don't know where the guns are," she said with a raised voice. "I didn't even know Kid was dealing them."

"You know, Ruby," Sonny said. "Don't lie to me."

"I don't! You have to believe me."

Backing up, Sonny turned with one last spine-chilling look and walked to a car parked on the street, a driver waiting there.

Ruby went back inside, agitated, frustrated and scared. She saw Maya had noticed her disappearance. She stood by the front door, a questioning look in her eyes.

Where did you go?

Nowhere, Ruby signed back. *Someone stopped by to talk. They're gone now.*

I'm hungry, Maya signed.

"Okay. Let's get you fed." Ruby signed along with speaking aloud. Then she walked into the kitchen and began preparing lunch. All the while she kept mulling over what to do about Santiago. She had to find a safe place for Maya, and the only thing that came to mind was Damon.

Settling her daughter down at the table, Ruby cleaned up and stepped into the living room. Seeing the front blinds open, she went to close them. As she reached for the cord, she saw a familiar car parked on the street. Cigarette smoke floated up from the driver's window.

Ruby closed the blinds, shaken. They would be watching her all the time now. Unsettled, she didn't feel she had much of a choice. She could go to the police, maybe call Sean, but legally what could they do but stop by and check things out? She didn't want to impose on Sean and January. They had done enough for her.

Back in the kitchen, Maya had finished her lunch. She got her daughter's attention.

I need you to go pack a bag, Maya. We're going to stay with Damon for a while.

Maya's whole face lit up, and she laughed. Ruby loved the sound. But she adored Damon way too much. Her attachment to the man bothered Ruby. It also touched a deep spot in her heart where she had no control. She just had to stay focused. Maya's safety was a number-one priority. She would take her to Damon, at least temporarily, until she figured out another option.

Taking her cell to her own bedroom, she called Damon.

"Are you all right?" Damon asked when he answered.

"Yes, but one of Kid's men just stopped by asking about guns and ammo."

"Who?"

"Sonny."

"Damn. That's not good, Ruby." Damon sounded tense with concern.

"I know."

"Please come and stay with me," he said.

"That's why I called. Is it all right if we stay there until we find another safe place?" she asked.

Silence met her across the wireless connection. "You can stay here for as long as you need to," he finally said.

"Damon?" She said his name unbidden, her trepidation showing. She couldn't take it back now.

"I know, Ruby. Let's get you somewhere safe, and then we'll take it from there. I understand you don't trust me personally, but please trust me as a DEA agent."

His words rang true with her. This wasn't personal. She and Maya were in danger. "Okay."

"Just come to the bar. I have an extra key to my place."

Ruby ended the call, anxious to be gone from there and not alone and scared.

Damon watched Santiago sitting at a table with Orlando, Curtis and Sonny. Orlando's dead stare showed no emotion as he looked from Curtis to Sonny. As the leader of the lesser ranked members of Santiago's organization, he exuded an aura of evil power. Curtis was the weaker of the members, shorter in height and a man of few words. Sonny was much more dangerous, a powder keg of easily triggered temper.

Earlier he had spoken to Sonny and Curtis and the two had left. Damon wondered where they had gone and hoped it wasn't to harass Ruby. Now Santiago and Orlando seemed to be having a chummy conversation.

Sonny and Curtis reappeared at the pub, going to the table and sitting. Sonny spoke to Santiago, who nodded in satisfaction. Then he looked over at Damon. Standing, he walked to the bar and took a stool.

"How are you today, Damon?" Santiago asked.

"I can't complain. And you?"

"I am well, except for my missing guns and ammunition."

Damon nodded.

"Have you made any progress with your girlfriend?"

"If you mean does she know anything about that, no. I asked her, and she doesn't know anything." Would his word be enough?

"My friend Sonny over there doesn't agree. He stopped by to talk with her, and she denied knowing anything to him as well, but he thinks she isn't telling the truth."

Great. Now they were going to turn up the heat on Ruby? No wonder she'd called and said she was on her way. At least he knew she was all right. Just scared, most likely. He'd do his best to make her feel safe.

"What if she is telling the truth?" Damon asked.

"That's what I need you to find out. Are you still seeing her?"

"Yes. In fact, she's going to come and stay with me now." Damon looked Santiago straight in the eyes.

"Ah. Then, things are progressing? She should be able to trust you to give you information. See that she does. Do we understand each other?"

"Yes, I believe we do." But did Santiago and his men understand that Damon would kill any one of them if they put so much as one finger on Ruby?

"She's only afraid someone will come after her if she tells them she knows where the items are. I don't want to harm her. I only want my guns."

His guns. That was priceless. He wasn't the one who'd bought them on the black market. "I'll do my best."

"You should do better than that, my friend. If you can't get her to talk, I will have to take matters into my own hands."

"Ruby can't reveal what she doesn't know, Santiago. I believe her. I can tell she isn't lying about that. She doesn't know."

Santiago leaned forward and patted Damon's shoulder. "Then, you will find a way to get me my guns and ammo, won't you?"

Now he expected Damon to magically produce guns? He shouldn't be surprised. A thug like him didn't listen to reason.

"I plan on giving you a sizable cut from the sale of them," Santiago said.

"Well, that certainly gives me some inspiration. You can count on me."

"I knew I could." Santiago glanced around. "I haven't seen Ruby here. Are you sure the two of you are doing all right? Sonny said you haven't been with her every day like you usually are."

"We're fine."

"When she gets here, I'd like to meet her."

He wanted to meet Ruby? Certainly not for personal reasons. Santiago was no friend. He wanted one thing from Ruby and one thing only. Guns. And he expected Damon to deliver. Even if Damon had to snap his fingers to make them appear.

"All right," Damon said.

With that, Santiago stood and walked like a man who believed he controlled the world. Damon would work very hard to arrest them all before any of them could hurt Ruby.

On the way to the Foxhole, Ruby alternated between looking in the rearview mirror at Maya playing with a doll and driving and watching for suspicious cars. So far she hadn't been followed. It was almost four in the afternoon. She just wanted to get to Damon's home and feel safe.

Ruby's cell rang. Seeing it was January, she answered, putting the phone on speaker.

"Just checking up on you," January said.

"I'm fine." Ruby wished no one had seen her that night.

"You left so upset. I'm going to be looking in on you from time to time."

"Well, you'll have to look in on me at Damon's

apartment above the bar." Might as well get that out in the open.

"Wha—" January was clearly stunned. "You two patched things up?"

"No, not really." Not by a long shot. "Kid's men have been coming around, giving me veiled threats. I'm staying with Damon for Maya's sake." That was a partial truth. She truly did think he was her best bet for survival. "I would have called Sean, but it's Damon's case. He's more familiar with it and everyone he's been investigating."

"No need to explain. I'm thrilled."

She was?

"I don't pretend to know Damon super well, but what I do know so far is he's got a lot of integrity. Did you know he and his brothers and I think his cousins are going to help us fight Carin and her penchant for ruining Colton Connections?"

"No." He was going to do that?

"I don't mean to say anything bad about his dad and uncle, but it's just the way they're going about it, attacking us."

"Damon doesn't seem to have a close relationship with his father," Ruby said. "In fact, he grew up wanting to be the opposite of him."

January smiled and nodded. "I believe that. Hotshot, handsome DEA agent."

"You have Sean."

"Yes. They do share some similarities. I can't tell you how grateful we are that Damon and his brothers are going to help. I just don't want Erik and Axel to cost my entire family everything they've worked so hard to build. What they are trying to get will literally take everything from us."

"I heard about it," Ruby said. Hearing Damon had redeemable qualities went against her new perception of him. She had believed he did. She didn't feel like forgiving him yet but felt this was the wisest move to make at the moment.

Ruby arrived at the Foxhole. The dining area and bar was about half-full. She spotted Damon serving drinks, and his rugged good looks struck her. Somehow knowing he fought for justice made him more attractive to her. She wouldn't share that with him, though.

Ruby took Maya's hand, and they walked toward the bar. She was a little uncomfortable bringing her daughter into a place like this, but the Foxhole was more of a pub and not run-down. She hoped it wouldn't trigger some dormant memory and upset her. She seemed to be doing fine, looking around and studying people as she often did.

Damon saw her approach and finished with a customer. He said something to another bartender, who nodded. Then Damon walked from behind the bar and came to stand before her.

"Hi, Maya," he said.

Maya signed *hello* back with a big smile.

Then Damon surprised her by leaning in to kiss her mouth. "We need to make it look believable." His voice was low, breath falling against her skin.

They had to make it appear as though they were seeing each other? Why? Part of his cover, no doubt.

"I need to introduce you to Santiago," Damon said. "Are you up for that?"

Ruby wasn't a liar. Her face revealed too much. "No, I'm not up for that!"

"All right. Let's get you both settled in, and then you can come back down later." He glanced over at Santiago as though worried they'd create an unpleasant scene.

Ruby became angry. "I'm not acting, Damon." She was well aware of her stance, but he had to understand he couldn't just turn on a switch in her and have her do his bidding.

He met her gaze. "You're right, Ruby, but we can't afford probing questions right now."

Maya tugged at her hand, and Ruby saw her worried face.

It's all right, Ruby signed.

Damon put his hand on her lower back and led her and Maya toward a back door. Through that was a storage area, and on the far left was a heavy wooden door. Damon punched in a code and opened it for her and Maya.

"I'll give you the code. Don't write it down anywhere."

He was in commando mode.

Inside the door was a remarkably clean and bright entry. A console had a vase of silk flowers. There were no windows. An intricately trimmed staircase turned to the left after three steps to a landing, where more stairs led to the second level.

Pictures of cities hung on the wall. Chicago, of course. New York. London and Paris.

Ruby was impressed. She was even more impressed when she reached the top of the stairs where another landing offered plenty of room for entry. Not only that, she could barely hear the noise from the pub.

She supposed gangs liked nice places, too. This wasn't a dress-to-the-nines establishment, but it seemed solidly constructed.

Damon opened the door for her and Maya.

As they entered she was again surprised. The apartment was like a warehouse, a loft conversion, with tall ceilings and open space. Two sitting areas, one with a huge television, and a modern kitchen with an island, and a dining room. She saw a hall to the left in the middle of the space. That must be the bedrooms and bathroom. There was another bathroom right off the entry.

"Wow. This is nice."

"I do have my standards."

Ruby heard his sarcasm and looked back at where he stood unable to suppress a soft smile.

His grin disarmed her so she focused on the accommodations. "Where will you have me and Maya?"

"Maya can have her own room, or you can stay in the same one," he said. "Let me show you."

He walked down the hall, and she took in everything. The clean white trim, the wood-floored bathroom with an open shelf of towels. The first bedroom burst with cheerful colors and a queen bed.

Maya made a gleeful sound and jumped up onto the bed with her backpack.

"Well, I guess this is your room," Ruby said, putting Maya's suitcase down.

"You have your own room," Damon said. "There

are three bedrooms." He walked down the hall to a door opposite another.

Ruby went there. This room was decorated in softer tones, more of a seashell theme.

"Did you do all this?" she asked.

"It came furnished."

"It's nice for being above a pub named the Foxhole." She put down her suitcase on the bed. "Quiet, too."

"The owner told me it was constructed to be soundproof. He originally lived here with his family before they bought a house."

Lucky her. This would be a good place for a kid, away from the adult atmosphere downstairs. Ruby appreciated that.

"We need to go down and talk with Santiago," Damon said. "I called January, and she agreed to come over and watch Maya."

He must have done that after she had spoken with January and before she'd arrived at the Foxhole. January was probably the only person she would trust with her daughter, other than her mother. How thoughtful of Damon to choose her. January could sign.

"Why is it so important I meet him?" she asked.

"He asked to meet you. I told him I asked you to stay with me. I wasn't sure you would."

In other words, Santiago was not a man to be disappointed. Kid had been the same way. She had discovered that abhorrent thing about him too late.

The buzzer by the door went off. January was here. Ruby followed Damon to the door, where he pressed an intercom button and checked his phone. His doorbell was equipped with a camera.

"Hello, January."

She smiled and waved at the camera. "Hello."

Damon let her through the lower door. Ruby was impressed by the security. Like a big apartment building, he could buzz people in from inside his apartment, and he must have a security system in place. She looked up and saw a detector at the top of the door. She spotted other devices throughout the room, motion detectors.

Damon allowed January inside, and her beautiful smiling face appeared.

"Thank you for coming on such short notice," Ruby said.

"Oh, no problem. I feel lucky that I get to spend time with Maya," she said, hugging Ruby.

Ruby stepped back.

"Are you two going on a date?" January asked, moving farther into the home, looking around, presumably for Maya.

"Sort of," Damon said. "I want to introduce her to some people."

"Mercer's group?" January asked, clearly perplexed.

"Santiago made the request. But we shouldn't be talking about that," Damon said.

"Of course. I know the drill."

Sean was a cop, so she must be accustomed to the irregular hours and complexity of police work.

"Where's Maya?" January asked.

"She's in her room, probably already has her toys spread out. She loves going to new places."

January laughed fondly. "She's a very brave girl." She continued to look around, taking in the apartment.

"This is a lovely home, Damon. It has a…family kind of feel to it."

"A family did live here before me," he said.

"He's being modest. Maya likes him," Ruby said, looking at Damon and saying with some angst, "a lot."

"What's not to like?" January said. "She liked Sean, too. It's good she's got some good men in her life to influence her."

Damon grinned at Ruby, probably loving the vote of confidence.

Okay. Enough of that. "Let's get this over with." Ruby stepped to the door.

Just then, Maya came out of her bedroom. Seeing January, her eyes brightened, and a big smile sprang forth.

January signed, *Hi, Maya.*

Maya reached out to her, and January crouched to take her into her arms. They hugged for a moment. Then January leaned back and smoothed Maya's hair back from her face.

"Look how pretty you're getting," January said.

Come play dolls with me, Maya signed.

January straightened and looked from Damon to Ruby. "I've been summoned."

Ruby laughed, adoring her daughter. "We shouldn't be long. Can you stay for dinner? I know Maya would love that."

"Why, yes. I'll definitely take you up on that. Mind if I invite Sean?"

"Not at all."

Maya took January's hand and tugged her.

"Don't worry about us," January said, looking back as she walked with Maya toward the bedroom.

Smiling, Ruby led Damon down the stairs. At the bottom, he stopped her.

She looked up at him in question.

"This is going to be tricky, Ruby. I need to make sure you're ready."

"I'm ready. Don't worry." She didn't have to pretend to be attracted to him, if that's what bothered him.

"We have to appear to be a real couple."

"I know. We can exchange a look here and there, and you can hold my hand," she said.

"If I touch you, are you going to recoil?" he asked.

She wouldn't like that, but it was necessary, she supposed. "No. I'll play along, but only for Maya, to keep her safe."

"I think we should practice," he said.

"Practice what?"

"A kiss?"

Ruby stepped back. "We don't have to go that far, do we?"

"I hope not, but just in case..."

She eyed him, wondering if he was trying to maneuver his way back into her heart. He was already there, but she didn't need any more temptation.

"It's just to be sure, Ruby," he said, as though reading her.

After a moment more of thought, she finally nodded. "All right." She didn't want to blow this any more than he did.

Gently, he slid his arm around her and pulled her against him. The shock of her body against his startled her. The potency of her attraction and desire disconcerted her.

"Easy," he murmured, sexy and deep.

Her inner turmoil must show. When he moved his head closer, her heart flew. His lips pressed to hers.

Ruby tensed and tried to shove him away. It was too much. Too strong.

He released her, his brow went low with displeasure. "See, now that's the kind of thing that could get us both killed."

Ruby stepped back. "I never asked to be a part of your *investigation*, Damon. This is not who I am. It's who you are."

"No, you never asked, but you were a part of it from day one. Whether you knew it or not, you were a part of it. Your association with Kid put you in this situation, not me. What do you think would have happened if I hadn't been sent here to work undercover?"

She shivered with what he was suggesting. She and Maya would be in so much danger. She had felt in danger even after Kid was killed.

"I see your point. It's just..." She couldn't bring herself to voice again his betrayal.

"I know, Ruby." Damon's expression relaxed. He put his hands on her shoulders. "I'm well aware you don't want me to touch you and you'd rather not be near me. Let's just play our roles and resolve this case. Then... then we can take it from there."

She didn't dislike being near him. That was actually a problem. She did like being with him, which wasn't good for her. She was still too out of sorts over the way he played her. Had he felt the same as her, or had he pretended? She didn't know what to believe. The way he said they'd take it from where the investigation left off gave her tickles of butterflies inside, but her mind was full of caution.

That set aside, they had to get through this evening safely, and that meant convincing Santiago their relationship was real…even if it wasn't.

"All right." She slid her hands up his chest to his shoulders. "Let's try that again." She rose up and kissed his mouth, then lowered and looked up at him with her best *I'm attracted to you* face. "How was that?"

His eyes smoldered. "Good." He stepped back. "A little too good." She smiled and went through the door. Damon followed but walked beside her once they appeared in the restaurant and bar. She recognized Sonny, who sat at a table with two other men. She presumed the older man was Santiago. He looked over as they approached.

She stopped next to Damon at the table.

"Ruby Duarte?" the man said.

"That's me." Ruby smiled, having to force it. These people were no different than Kid.

The man stood and extended his hand. "Santiago. Damon has told me a lot about you."

"Has he?" Ruby glanced over at Damon. Only he could read her thoughts. He'd talked a lot about her because she was an integral part of his investigation.

"All good, of course." Santiago smiled, and for a moment he could pass as an ordinary, friendly guy. He turned to his cohorts. "This is Orlando and Sonny."

"I've met Sonny before," she said tersely, then in greeting she said, "Orlando."

"Nice to meet you," Orlando said in a flat tone. His eyes were beady brown and dead. No doubt, he was a scary man.

"Nice to see you again, Ruby," Sonny said a little snidely.

"Please. Have a seat. Join us," Santiago said.

Ruby bet he was not this congenial most of the time. Kid had been the same way, playing nice when in reality he was an extremely dangerous man. She sat beside him, Damon to her right at the round table, one of the largest in the dining area.

The men went about talking business for what seemed an endless length of time. Santiago and his men talked about nothing that had any bearing on her safety, just a lot of bragging as far as she could tell. She checked the clock on a nearby wall and saw more than thirty minutes had passed.

When she faced them again, she noticed they all looked at her and their conversation had stopped.

"Damon tells me you work at a bookstore with a coffee shop?" Santiago said.

"Yes. And attending college for nursing," she said.

"Ah. A woman with a caring heart. No wonder Damon kept going back for your coffee."

Ruby smiled at Damon, who met her eyes with warming energy passing between them. That she didn't have to fake. She wondered if he did.

Turning back to Santiago, she saw that he had noticed the exchange and seemed skeptical.

"We were all saddened by Kid's death," he said. "He was a friend and a hard worker. Loyal."

Loyal. Ruby smothered a scoff. Loyal in breaking the law.

"Kid told me you left him a few years before that," Santiago said.

What was he getting at? Why was all of this important? "Yes."

"And he kept your daughter."

"Against my will, yes, he did. He forbade me from seeing her, although I tried." Ruby could not pretend she had obeyed or gone along with that. She glanced at Orlando, whose expression apparently never changed. Sonny eyed her smugly.

"I will say that he was upset you left. Heartbroken."

Really? He'd had an awful way of showing that.

"Keeping your daughter was probably his way of lashing out. It was an emotional reaction," Santiago said. "I hope someday you can forgive him. I realize having a child taken from you is difficult, but know that it isn't something Kid took lightly."

Difficult? The man was insane. Difficult didn't begin to describe what she had gone through. And Kid deserved no forgiveness. Kid may not have *taken it lightly*, but he had done it out of spite and viciousness.

"She's getting past that, and Maya is doing very well," Damon said.

He must have sensed her steaming reaction.

"This is good," Santiago said. "I was beginning to wonder if the two of you were parting ways."

Ruby stewed inside. They'd been spying on her for a long time, and she had never known. She had suspected, that's all. She'd wanted more than anything to rid herself of Kid. Permanently. Even dead, he still terrorized her.

"I'm sorry," she said. "Why would you think that? And why would it matter?"

Under the table, Damon tapped her foot with his.

Santiago's entire demeanor changed. Ruby saw the evil emerge in his eyes and the way he leaned back in his chair and drove his gaze into hers.

"I don't think I need to explain that to an intelligent women such as yourself," he said. "But now that you mention it, we noticed the two of you weren't together last Saturday and weren't together after that until now. It's suspicious."

So he was the couples police on top of drug slash arms dealer? Why did he care? His weapons, of course, but why was it important for Ruby and Damon to be together? Because he thought Damon was playing her and he'd have a better chance of getting her to talk?

"Where did you go that night?" Santiago asked.

Ruby checked her rising ire and indignation. This was where Damon would tell her their lives depended on how she answered.

"I was invited to a party," she said.

"And you didn't take Damon?"

"We're just dating," Damon said.

"Yes, just dating, but you, Damon, weren't home that night, either. Where did you go?"

That told Ruby he'd had someone follow her and probably had someone watching Damon, but he had made sure he wasn't tailed. Santiago knew she had ties with the Coltons.

Good lord, this was getting diabolical. And way, way too dangerous.

"I went to see a friend," he said.

"Who's the friend?"

"Someone I've known since high school. He lives in California and came out to see his family. We spent some time together."

Ruby forced herself not to look at Damon. He was such a good liar. He sounded calm and confident, and seeing Santiago's face confirmed he believed him.

After a time, Santiago turned to Ruby. "I trust Damon's intentions, but I have trouble with yours."

The sting of fear shot through her. "I'm not sure I understand what you mean."

"I mean… Kid took your daughter from you. Have you infiltrated yourself into Damon's life in some sort of plot to have revenge?"

Her breath whooshed out of her.

"She didn't know me before I went to get coffee," Damon said.

"Yes, yes. I know. But once she knew where you worked, she might have devised a plan."

Oh, geez. That was so ridiculous. Ruby hoped her cynicism didn't show.

"She had no plan. She only wants to be rid of Kid and anyone associated with him. She lives in fear every day." Damon turned a pointed look toward Sonny.

Santiago smiled, and not with any humor. "That is good to hear." He met Ruby's eyes, which she was sure were hard and direct right now. "Since you don't know where my guns and ammo are, perhaps your daughter does?"

That was enough. Ruby shot to her feet. "How dare you!"

Santiago flattened his hands on the table, and his face grew ominous. "How dare I? How dare you speak to me that way!"

"You're suggesting my daughter was involved in what Kid was doing," Ruby said, not softening her tone at all for this reprobate.

Damon stood and took her hand. "Ruby?"

She glanced at him, incensed that he would allow this man to threaten her little girl.

"Not involved. I merely said she might have seen something."

While that might be true, Ruby would not stand for Santiago drawing Maya into any dangerous situation.

"She's *five years old*!" Ruby spat out at Santiago.

Santiago continued to regard her as though at any moment he would signal his men to take her out. "I am aware. But she was with Kid in his last years. You were not. She may have seen something. Perhaps you can ask her."

"I will do no such thing." Not the way he likely pictured that playing out. Ruby wouldn't ask her daughter where Kid hid a stash of weapons.

"My advice to you now is to consider very carefully how you proceed, Ms. Duarte."

Meaning she had better do as he asked or he might take matters into his own hands—take her daughter from her as Kid had done. That infuriated her.

She stepped around the table and leaned down, putting her face close to Santiago's. "If you or your men go anywhere near my daughter, I'll kill you," she hissed.

Santiago looked up at her face, his anger having faded. Now he only looked amused. He turned to his men, who had put their hands on their weapons, exposing them for her to see. With a shake of his head, his men concealed their guns.

Santiago looked at Damon. "She's a pistol, this one. But then, I shouldn't be surprised, given she was with Kid."

"You'll have to excuse her. She's very protective of Maya. We'll see what we can do, though. You have my word," Damon said.

He walked to her and took her arm in a gentle but firm grasp. "Let's go, Ruby." Then he turned to Santiago. "Until we meet again."

Ruby fumed inside, but she knew better than to incite a man like Santiago any further. She left with Damon, itching to have it out with him. She didn't havc to wait long...

Chapter 8

At the door requiring a code, Damon took Ruby's arm and gently turned her to face him. Leaning down and close to her face, he said sternly, "What were you *thinking* talking to him like that?"

He got it that she understood he had his cover to preserve, and she probably thought he had to understand she would not budge when it came to Maya. He didn't blame her for that. She'd lived around these thugs. She knew what they were capable of. She also knew the only language they listened to was violence.

"Anyone who even implies a threat to Maya will know my wrath," she said in an equally terse tone.

Letting go of her, he pinched the bridge of his nose. After he calmed himself, he lowered his hand and looked at her.

"Ruby, I'm not in the habit of letting pieces of work like Santiago run me, but I'm undercover here. The way you behave and the way you speak to a man like that could trigger his psychopathic nature. He's a violent narcissist. He could order you killed in an instant."

Ruby's head lowered. Then after a few seconds she lifted it and looked into his eyes. "I know. How can you possibly not realize that? I was with Kid Mercer."

Damon held his hands up. "Okay, yes. I do know that, but you aren't a professional in dealing with these people. You were a victim. I'm the guy who's trying to put an end to them all."

He could see her concession. She agreed. And maybe she even liked what he said about ending them. Ending the violence. Ending their terror on innocent people. Damon's number-one goal was to stop it all. Hopefully, she liked that about *him*.

"You can't behave like that ever again," he said as gently as he could. She was a mama bear when it came to Maya, maybe even more so than most moms given her history.

"What do you want me to do?" she asked.

"No disagreeing or showing your abhorrence for the man. Never forget that I'm on your side."

She eyed him dubiously.

"Trust me, Ruby. Trust me as a DEA agent. If you can't trust me as an ordinary man, trust me as an agent."

Her doubt and distrust eased, he saw. And she said, "Okay. Deal."

Geez, this was going to be harder than he thought. Ruby was no pushover. A little transparent in an unabashed way. She never internalized what people thought of her. She had her thoughts and owned them. Her expressions gave her away because she didn't care to hide them. She was about as honest as a woman could be, which both endeared him and raised his defenses. He had thought Laurel was honest, too.

Entering the apartment, Damon saw Sean had arrived and both he and January were in the kitchen, fresh vegetables strewn over the counter and something delicious cooking. Maya saw them from her perch on the kitchen island and jumped down to rush to her mother. Ruby swooped her up and held her in a smiling hug. Then leaned back to look at her daughter's sweet face. Ruby kissed her nose.

"I love you," she said.

Love, Maya signed.

Ruby carried Maya to the kitchen and put her down. "It smells great in here."

Making fried chicken and mac and cheese, Maya signed, excited.

"Oven-fried," January said.

A little healthier. But kid-friendly.

"Also a salad and some mashed potatoes," Sean said. He wore an apron that matched January's.

"Did Sean bring the aprons?" Ruby asked.

"He brought everything to make dinner. We decided together." January looked at Sean and the two shared a warm exchange.

Damon thought how nice it would be to have that with a woman. While he felt he might be able to have that with Ruby, he had been through relationships in the past where he'd believed the same and ended up being wrong. So for now, he simply envied a couple who had found that rare love, shared by both. Damon didn't consider himself lucky in love. Especially with Ruby, at least right now.

When Ruby reached for the bowl of salad, Sean playfully swatted her hands away.

"Go sit down," he said. "This is our treat tonight."

Ruby laughed. "What did we do to deserve such pampered treatment?"

Damon enjoyed watching her easy charm and the way she moved, so graceful. Her figure didn't go unmissed, either. He always admired her shape. She had nice legs, long and fit in leggings today with a blouse that fell to just below her waist.

She directed Maya to a chair at the table, and Damon joined them, sitting adjacent to Ruby. Sean and January brought the food and soon they were all preparing plates, Ruby helping Maya with hers.

"When January told me you lived here, I got a little curious." Sean broke the silence other than the sounds of the process of eating.

Damon chewed some chicken and looked at him. He was always careful about his undercover work, but with his identity blown with Ruby and her connection to his family, he had no choice but to take a risk. Sean and January knew enough already, with Sean being a cop who'd worked a case involving Mercer. As a cop, Sean was no dummy. It hadn't taken much for him to ascertain the reason Damon was living here, above the Foxhole. He probably already knew Mercer's gang hung out in the pub.

"Don't worry, we know the drill. We won't say anything to anyone." Sean glanced over at January.

"Nope," she said.

It was no secret Sean was well aware of Kid Mercer and his followers. "I'd rather not talk about it," Damon said.

"I had the distinct pleasure of meeting Santiago tonight—playing my new role." Ruby turned a caustic gaze to Damon.

"I had to introduce her to the new leader downstairs." Santiago. He looked at Ruby. "It didn't go so well."

Ruby shoved her food around on her plate. "He started to ask if Maya knew anything about what her father did, and I got upset."

January's brow lifted. "Understandably so."

Damon didn't blame her for that, either, as he'd already concluded during their meeting with Santiago. He only wanted her safe. Maya safe. It drove him to anxiety sometimes. What if he couldn't protect them? She'd fight Santiago with all her might, but by herself she'd fail. Damon had spent months infiltrating Mercer's organization. She knew what they were capable of, but protecting her daughter might cloud her judgment.

"If you need any help, I've got experience with Mercer," Sean said.

That wasn't a mystery to Damon. "Thanks. I just might take you up on that. You've heard of Santiago?"

Sean glanced around. "Is this place bugged?"

"No." Damon grinned. "I sweep it regularly."

Sean nodded, clearly relating to Damon as an undercover operative. "Yes, I've heard of Santiago. Not the most congenial gent."

"Oh, he can put up a facade," Ruby said, scooping up a bite of mac and cheese at the same time Maya did, who giggled as she chewed.

"He says Mercer had a stash of armaments and has pretty much said Ruby knows where it is, whether she does or not."

"Which I don't," Ruby said.

"He expects us to find it."

"He thinks Maya knows where it is." Ruby rolled her eyes, elbow on the table, fork hanging from her fingers. "They've been harassing me. After the party I came home to a note that said, *We're watching you.* Who does that?"

Suddenly Ruby stilled and turned to Damon. She had not told him that.

"What?" he demanded. "They sent you a note, and you didn't *tell* me?"

"I told you Sonny came to see me," she said. "That was more threatening than a note."

"Don't keep anything from me, Ruby," he said, exasperated. "Why didn't you think that was important?"

"It *was* important. I didn't want to scare Maya," she said.

Why did she have to do that? He would have done the same. Not talk about danger in front of an impressionable child. Or not want to frighten Damon, so as to alert her daughter to that danger. Whatever it might be, Ruby's foremost thoughts were of Maya.

"Please, Ruby. Find a way to tell me when things like that happen," he said.

Ruby poked her fork into what was left of her macaroni. "All right. I will. But it isn't as if you haven't kept anything from me."

Sean chuckled. "You just found out he's undercover."

Ruby turned an incensed gaze to him. "It's not funny."

Sean held his hand up. "I'm not laughing because of that. It's just...it's obvious the two of you were meant for each other."

Ruby's mouth dropped open, and she looked at Damon.

"What?" Ruby said, clearly shocked.

"Don't mind him," January said. "He means no harm. We both went through turbulent waters like you two are. And I have to agree, it is obvious you both have feelings for each other."

"January..." Ruby protested, sounding as though she might as well say, *I thought you were my friend.*

"Mmm, this chicken is sooo good." She ate a bite and then sat up straight, dropping her fork and uttering, "Oh." She put her hand on her belly.

Sean put his fork down, too, and met her eyes.

"The twins must like fried chicken, too." January laughed softly, and the exchange between her and Sean was palpable.

Damon was almost uncomfortable. He wanted that with a woman. That love. He looked over at Ruby, whose mouth had dropped open slightly as she stared at the marvelous spectacle.

Sean put his hand on January's stomach, and they shared the movements of their children. The world had obviously dropped away as they basked in ultimate and soul-consuming love.

Without thinking on it too much, Damon moved his hand to cover Ruby's. She had to know how significant this moment was.

He turned to her. She closed her mouth and met his gaze, clearly flustered but awed at the same time.

His feelings for her were too strong for his comfort, but he'd be a fool not to consider what a future with her would look like.

"Sean and I had our hurdles to jump, too. My advice is to take it a day at a time," January said.

Jarred from the exchange with Ruby, Damon turned to the couple.

Sean put his hand on January's on the table.

Damon was sure he'd looked at Ruby that way. She had looked at him that way, too. If only he could be certain that his heart was safe with her and that she felt the same about him.

January looked at Maya and then Ruby and both signed and said, "We have an announcement to make."

That changed the mood. What did they want to tell them?

"January's baby shower is coming up," Sean said and January kept signing for Maya.

Ruby sucked in a breath and stood from the table. She went around the table and hugged January.

"Oh, congratulations!" Ruby exclaimed. "I know what it meant to you to have Maya live with you and to have the adoption thwarted by my return. I'm so happy that you're having twins!"

"I'll always have a soft spot for Maya." January

looked at the girl fondly, signing that she would have twins.

Maya smiled big. She had crumbs on her mouth from the chicken she held in both hands.

"We're also eloping." January beamed.

Eloping? Damon couldn't believe it. He looked at Ruby and wondered if he ever had the opportunity to get her pregnant if she'd have a pair, too. Twins most certainly ran in this branch of the Coltons!

Ruby met his eyes and seemed to be wondering the same. Damon couldn't tell if it frightened her or if the idea tantalized her.

Ruby finished cleaning up after breakfast while Damon sat on the sofa with Maya. They had a Tinker Bell movie going, and Damon seemed genuinely into it. Maya sat close to him, snuggling. Damon had his arm across the back of the sofa and every once in a while looked down at what Maya was drawing in her art book. The two of them together tugged at her heartstrings. Kid had never been like that with their daughter. Maya had been more like a possession. He had been prouder of planting a seed than he had been of Maya as a little human being.

Damon moved his arm from the sofa and signed, *Wow, that is really good.*

Maya put her drawing book down and signed, *I love drawing.*

Are you going to grow up to be an artist?

Maya shrugged. *I don't know.*

Can I see what you've drawn so far? Then to Ruby he asked, "How long has she been drawing?"

"Ever since she could handle a crayon. That book is about a year old. She's had that through her therapy sessions. It's almost full now, though."

Maya gave him the book, and Damon started from the beginning.

Ruby walked over. It had been a while since she'd seen Maya's drawings. The first few were those an innocent girl would draw. Stick figures. Flowers. The sky, sun, dogs and a family. The family drawings sort of broke Ruby's heart. They were so idyllic. Nothing like what it had been with Kid, and then after when he had prevented Ruby from seeing her own daughter.

Then the drawings grew darker. Maya had created them after she had been found in a warehouse where three of Kid's gangers had been shot and killed. One of the men was helping to bring Kid down, and it was assumed the three were killed before they could talk.

Some of Maya's drawings were of what appeared to be a warehouse. Others were of her home but were all in dark shades, with evil-looking faces in a window or peeking up over a bed, all drawn like a five-year-old's rendition, cartoonish and sometimes difficult to decipher. Her therapist had used them in some of her sessions.

Maya became engrossed in the movie while Damon turned pages. He came to one that had the recurring theme of a warehouse, this one with stickmen holding Ls as if depicting a gun. One had red lines shooting out of it. Ruby had been enormously disturbed that her daughter had drawn images of men shooting guns.

"She drew these just after I got her back," Ruby

said. "It was when she was going through therapy. She never mentioned anything to the therapist."

"What do you mean? These look like guns," Damon said.

"They are, but Maya never elaborated on them. I don't think she wanted to talk about what she saw that night the three men were killed."

The next drawing was another warehouse, dark and foreboding from the mind of a troubled little girl, trouble her father had caused by merely being Kid Mercer. This one depicted more stickmen but had a table with what appeared to be a mound of guns. Maya had drawn what Ruby and the therapist had surmised was a puddle of blood under the table.

"I don't like looking at these," Ruby said. "I tried to take the book away from her, but she wouldn't let me. She keeps saying she isn't finished yet." Her drawings had gotten much better since she had drawn these, and Maya didn't go back to look at them. She only enjoyed drawing new pictures. Ruby thought it was remarkable that her daughter didn't like waste. She had to draw on every page before getting a new book.

The next few pictures were of mounds of Ls, some big, some small. In one, there was more than one table.

"These piles of guns seem important," Damon said. "It's almost as if the shooting she saw in the warehouse triggered other memories of guns."

Ruby leaned closer. Maya had drawn several piles of guns. In the next picture, the piles were accompanied by squares, possibly representing boxes.

Damon looked up at her. "Do you think Maya could have seen piles of guns and boxes of ammo?"

Ruby contemplated him. She did not want Maya involved in his investigation in any way. But if she had seen the guns and ammo…

"I suppose so."

Damon glanced at Maya, who was still into her movie, then back at Ruby. "Look, I would never put Maya in any situation that would be dangerous or traumatize her in any way, but if she did see something, maybe she can tell us where."

Ruby considered that, appreciating that he had addressed the possible impacts on Maya. She wasn't sure what seeing these places again would do to her.

"Santiago will never know it was her who led us to it," Damon said.

That was certainly a plus. If a man like Santiago discovered Maya had drawn pictures of a stockpile of guns, there was no telling what he would do to get the little girl to reveal the location. As far as he was concerned, Damon and Ruby were searching for the weapons. He would never know.

After weighing the consequences, Ruby nodded. "All right. Let's ask her about these pictures."

Damon touched Maya's shoulder. She reluctantly turned from the television and looked at him.

He pointed to the piles of guns and then waited for her eyes to lift. *Do you remember drawing these?* he signed.

Maya looked down at the picture again, then at her mother, seeming suddenly withdrawn and uncertain.

It's all right, Maya. You can tell him.

Maya turned to Damon and nodded.

Damon signed, *Is it a real place?*

Maya nodded. And lowered her head. Clearly she didn't like thinking about this.

Ruby touched her chin. "It's okay, Maya. You're safe. Damon is just…" She signed *curious.*

Are all the places you drew real? Damon signed. *You've been to them?*

Maya nodded.

Did you see these guns? Damon asked.

Again, she nodded. Damon looked sharply at Ruby.

It's what Daddy always had. And his friends, Maya signed.

Ruby pointed to one of the piles. *Where did you see them?* Maya didn't seem as reluctant now, so Damon thought she was all right with talking about it.

Maya stared at it a while and then looked up at her mother. *I don't remember.*

Okay. That's okay. Thank you. You can watch your movie now.

Maya seemed glad to do just that, and soon she was absorbed in Tinker Bell's latest adventure.

Damon stood, and Ruby went into the dining area with him, where he faced her. "This could be our ticket out of this mess."

Ruby became agitated, her eyes worrying. "I hope you don't mean Maya could be our ticket out of this mess."

"No, of course not. But if she can recognize one of those buildings she drew, maybe we could find something."

"But I thought those men were shot and killed in a warehouse. If the guns were there, wouldn't Sean have found them?"

"Not if it's a different warehouse."

Maya had drawn different kinds of buildings. One looked like a warehouse and had been a recurring image. Others were just small rooms. Some even had childlike pictures hanging on the walls.

"The changing scenes tell me she was confused when she drew them, like she didn't know much about the place where she saw the guns," Ruby said.

"All right," he said. "We'll take this slowly. I don't want to rush her into bad memories, but maybe we could take her to some places that might resemble her drawings, places Kid would have gone," Damon said.

"All right. Let's start by researching the places Kid went, and then maybe tomorrow we can drive around."

"Okay." Damon kissed her forehead. "I promise to put Maya first no matter what." He looked over at the cute little girl with her single braid and honey-brown eyes.

Touched by the honesty she heard in his tone, Ruby took in his determined face and fell in love with him a little bit. Then an instant later, the notion of falling in love with him—or any man—frightened her.

Damon brought his laptop to the table, and Ruby sat next to him. He also had a notebook and pen, which he handed to her.

"Make a list of all the places you know of where Mercer went or might have gone," he said.

"Well, here. The Foxhole." She wrote that down.

"Santiago would have checked here already. The warehouse where Mercer's men were murdered is out, too."

"Okay." Ruby thought for a moment. "His nightclub."

"Santiago probably checked there, too," Damon said.

"He had meeting space there, his own private quarters. Maybe there was some kind of secret entrance in the basement or something," she said. "There's also a large shipping dock there, with storage areas."

"We can go there, just you and me. We don't need Maya to see that place again. We can drop her off at January and Sean's, whenever they're available."

Ruby smiled into his eyes. "You would make a really good dad."

The words tumbled out before she thought better of it. He looked into her eyes, and she felt him warming with the words.

"You're already a great mom," he murmured, this time angling his head and kissing her mouth.

Although brief and chaste, it packed an electrical punch Ruby had not yet felt with him. She should be jumping off the chair and telling him to never do that again. Instead, she stayed in the heavenly sensation only he could produce.

"Uh…um…" Ruby stammered.

Damon wore a seductive grin and his eyes heated, obviously enjoying her awkward moment. He must know what she felt.

"K-Kid also had a storage unit he never let me or anyone see," she said.

That statement cleared Damon's face of passion.

Ruby wrote *storage unit* on the paper. "And then, of course, there's his home." She tapped the pen gently against her chin. "His closest drug dealer was killed by a rival gang. Maybe he stashed them at his house. His name is Michael Wallace, and he had a wife. She might still live there."

"All right. Then, I'd have to find a way inside."

"We can go visit her. She knows of me. I could distract her while you look around."

"She wouldn't know there was a bunch of guns stored in her house?" Damon asked. "Maybe not if he hid them somewhere."

"I've never been to their house," Ruby said.

"We'll find it."

"He also had mistresses," Ruby said. "One of them might know where he put them, or have some ideas."

"Wouldn't Santiago already have spoken with them?" Damon asked.

"Maybe. And if he and his men searched, they didn't find any guns."

"Let's assume Santiago has already spoken with everyone close to Kid. No one knows where the guns are, so we can also assume that wherever they are, Kid is the only one who knew."

For the first time since finding out Kid's true character, Ruby felt confident she'd be able to put him behind her once and for all. She would be rid of him. For real. She wouldn't have to keep looking over her shoulder or always have it in the back of her mind that he—while he still lived—or one of his men would come after her. Kid and his men needed no good reason to take someone out. Even the slightest perception of disloyalty was enough to justify a kill.

And Damon would be the one to help her do that. She met his eyes, turning her head where they sat close at the table. She felt herself softening to him, knowing it could well be a big mistake. But would it be? What if he was right for her? What if he wasn't?

She could not be wrong again.

Damon stepped into Kid's nightclub, aptly named the Nightcrawler. Kid hadn't broadcast his ownership of the club much. That had to be due to his use of it as a cover and a way to launder money. Decorated in bright colors beneath dim lighting, it smelled like stale alcohol. Tall tables filled most of the space, with a dance floor and stage centered toward the back. There was one long bar on the left and a smaller one on the right. There were few people here, as it was early.

"We aren't open yet." A dark-haired man appeared from a door beside the stage. "Frank didn't lock the door back up when he came in."

Frank must be an employee. Damon took out his badge. "I'm from the DEA. I was wondering if you'd mind if we took a look around."

The man stopped before them. "What for?"

"Are you the manager?"

"Nick Hansen. I'm the new owner."

"Oh, good. I'm investigating Kid Mercer's criminal activities. I need to have a look around."

"I was told police already did that months ago."

"I know. I just want to look again. It would really help our case against the gang members."

"Sure. No problem. I can show you around."

"We'll be fine. Just appreciate you letting us take a look." Damon gave a nod of appreciation, and he and Ruby walked farther into the club.

"The offices are up those stairs." Ruby pointed to an L-shaped staircase.

Damon could see she didn't like being here again. She led him into an anteroom where two sets of double doors were. One led to Kid's old office.

"It used to be a lot gaudier," Ruby said.

The space was large and had three desks and neon beer signs. A sofa was to the side.

"He had velvet sofas, and there were swords on the walls," Ruby said, scoffing. "He thought he was so important."

"This must be difficult for you," Damon said.

Ruby walked around looking at the room. "It feels different now. Cleaner. Not evil."

Seeing her at peace, Damon started searching for secret doorways. There was a bookshelf vacant of books but no hidden door.

He searched the rest of the office and then the conference rooms, now empty save one.

"I'll take you to the basement." Ruby led him to a doorway he already knew had stairs going down. He had planned on going there next. Kid must have had his own private passageway to the basement from here, probably to the club level as well.

It was a dark, narrow stairway, lit only by low-wattage bulbs spaced far apart. Damon wondered if Kid had gotten a rise out of that, especially when he'd led targeted enemies this way.

They passed a keypad-locked door that must provide entry to the club and descended farther. At another keypad entry, Damon checked the handle. The door opened.

He shared a look with Ruby. Apparently the new owner had nothing to hide the way Kid had.

Damon found himself in a well-lit storage area. This was where the club kept their supplies. There were crates and boxes everywhere. He imagined how it might have been when Kid ran the place. Not much different when it came to operations. What he looked for were hidden doors or safes or floor passages. He overturned rugs and moved items on shelves. There was nothing.

"Next stop—the storage unit," Ruby said.

Hearing her sigh, Damon went to her. He drew her against him and brushed some wayward strands of hair off her smooth skin. She was so beautiful.

"Thank you," he said.

Her eyes quirked as though in confusion.

"For coming with me here," he said. "I don't like reminders of my past, either, so I know what this must be costing you."

She blinked a few times. "You have to stop doing that."

"Doing what?" he asked.

"Making me fall for you." She gave him a semi-firm shove.

He took the hint and stepped back, not missing the ground he had gained with her. They were walking into territory neither of them welcomed. Damon's heart directed him, as he was sure hers did, too.

Where it led them, only the brave could go. Damon had never been weak, and he suspected Ruby was of the same ilk. He hoped they both ended up on the same path.

Chapter 9

Ruby noticed Damon checking and rechecking to make sure they weren't seen when they left the Nightcrawler and drove to Kid's storage unit. Damon insisted they leave his car at the club and take a cab. He walked with her several blocks before hailing one, telling her only then that he had noticed Santiago had someone tailing them. This was part of the plan. He was no fool.

Ruby had to fight off the tingling sensation of arousal the whole time.

Kid had kept all of his haunts close. His club, the Foxhole, his home, the storage unit. Even his mistresses lived close to his center of business. He must have put them up on his dime. Funny—or not—Ruby hadn't cared then, and she cared even less now.

It was getting late in the afternoon. The storage business wasn't busy in the middle of the week. It was an older establishment, something that may have appealed to Kid. Quiet. Off the beaten path. Mom-and-pop.

Reaching the storage facility, The cab driver parked in front of the one Kid had rented. They got out. The facility manager was waiting for them. Damon had obtained a search warrant. So the manager opened the unit and rolled the door up. Damon found himself looking at plastic-wrapped crates.

When Ruby stepped forward, he stopped her.

"This is when we have to make it official." Damon took out his phone and called his boss. They'd go through everything and keep it secret until the investigation was over.

Afterward, Ruby looked one way and the other, watching for Kid's men to jump out of the shadows.

"We weren't followed," he said. "You're safe."

Her shoulders lowered as tension drained out of her muscles. "You're sure?" She wanted to feel relief, but fear hung on to her.

"Very. That's why we took a cab. Santiago knows we went to the club and nothing more."

"So he'll want to know where we were," she said.

"We were at the club," he said.

Sirens and lights were a heavenly welcome sound and sight.

Damon got Ruby away from the DEA team foraging in the discovery of drugs in Kid's storage unit. He hid his great disappointment that only drugs had been found, no armory. Although he was sure Ruby shared his sentiment, she was quiet, exhausted. He needed to get her back to his apartment. Their absence would not go unmissed by Santiago and his men.

He had the taxi driver drop them several blocks from the Nightcrawler. Ruby was clearly done. Emotionally and physically. Damon had called Sean, and he and January would keep Maya for the night. She would be safe there. Damon could not predict what might transpire tonight. Santiago would not know they had discovered the storage unit, but he would know they had vanished from the nightclub.

He hoped Ruby was up for his plan.

At the nightclub, Damon readily saw two of Santiago's men watching as they got into his used maroon Cadillac.

Expected.

Ruby didn't notice. He ushered her into the passenger seat and got behind the wheel. He watched the car follow them. It would take some clever driving, but he knew just the route.

Using his blinker, he turned left. The car followed.

"This isn't the way to your apartment," Ruby said.

"We have company." He looked in the rearview mirror, which compelled her to lean forward enough to see into the passenger-door mirror.

Damon made a right and then another immediate right. There was a parking garage, again another right, where he drove and sped up to maneuver the lane. This garage had two entrances. The other opened to another street. Damon drove there and made a right. The next left brought him back to the road he'd originally been on. He watched the rearview mirror. The other car never appeared.

"Wow, you're good," Ruby said.

Damon drove to the back of the Foxhole, and the two of them climbed out. It was getting late. Ruby yawned. It had been a long day for her. He wanted to get her into the apartment and pamper her. She made him want to do things like that for her. He adored even her yawns.

Eyeing her fondly, he opened the door for her. The sound of people in the pub told him the bar hadn't closed yet.

Inside, he stopped short with Ruby when he saw Santiago and Orlando standing near the lower apartment door, waiting for them.

"Where were you?" Santiago demanded.

Ruby glanced at Damon, and he sensed her trepidation.

"We went to Kid's club looking for your weapons," Damon said.

"I'm aware of that. Where did you go after that?"

Damon put his arm around Ruby. "We wanted to be alone."

"You can be alone here." Santiago moved closer, inspecting them, or more like trying to dissect them.

"Can we?" Damon said in challenge.

"You didn't tell me where you were going or what you planned to do. My men lost you," Santiago said.

Just then, Sonny walked through the door. "He lost me on purpose."

"Your car was at the nightclub, and you were nowhere to be seen."

"We took a cab," Damon said.

"Why?"

"Why do you think?"

Santiago stared hard at him. "If you are trying to dupe me, you are making a big mistake."

Releasing Ruby, Damon stepped closer to him, standing a couple of inches taller. "Look, I don't like being followed. You said you want your guns—I'll get your guns, but you're going to have to call off your dogs."

Santiago glanced at Orlando with a nod.

Orlando moved on Ruby before Damon could predict what he would do. She gave a shriek as he grabbed her and put her back against him, holding a knife to her throat.

Ruby's eyes widened in terror.

Damon looked at Santiago. "Let her go." He swore he'd end this whole charade right now if he hurt Ruby. He was already afraid he'd do just that, if provoked. And Damon didn't think it would take much provocation for a man like him.

"This is what will happen if you do not cooperate, Damon. I'll take what you value from you. I want to know where you are and what you are doing at all times."

"Fine. Let's schedule a status update once a week like the corporate people do," Damon said. He had to fight to keep his cool. He'd accommodate the man, but Santiago also had to know he was no coward and he was not afraid of him or his men. "I'm sick of being followed. Stop tailing me."

Santiago held his gaze in that same deadly way. Then he looked at Orlando with another nod.

He released Ruby, and she ran to Damon, who held her to him. He took her hand and guided her in front of him toward the door.

"I want a status report at the end of the week," Santiago said.

"You know how to find me." Damon entered the code, careful to conceal it from Santiago and his men.

Inside, Ruby's head fell against his chest, and she breathed deeply a few times. "I was scared out of my mind."

"I wouldn't let anything happen to you. Santiago knows if anything happens to you now, he will never get his guns. He's just having a control-freak moment. And unfortunately, scare tactics are his way of maintaining that."

Ruby looked up at him, doubtful and tired. Damon realized she wasn't physically tired. She was tired of dealing with the fallout of Kid Mercer.

He understood now why she had so readily agreed to let Maya stay with January and Sean. Her number-one priority was Maya: she could not be exposed to anything relating to Kid's debauchery.

"Hey." Damon took her hands in his. "Maya is safe tonight. Let's get you relaxed."

Seeing the distressed response in her eyes, Damon held her hand and took her up the stairs. At the top he opened the door and ushered her in. Then he locked them inside.

"Go get comfortable," he told her. "I'm going to check the security system."

While she went to her bedroom, he did a security sweep and set the alarm. They were all alone tonight. Safe.

Ruby ran a bath in the main bathroom. She found some stress-relieving bubble bath and poured an ample amount in the warm water. Damon had been sensitive to her low bandwidth for Kid's criminality. She was so grateful Maya was with January tonight. She was at her limit of endurance. Please, could she just get Kid out of her life?

She wasn't sure if Damon had put candles in here on purpose, but they worked magic on her nerves, along with the vanilla-scented bubbles. The flickering flames offered the only light, which she loved. She rested her head back on a bath pillow and closed her eyes to ecstasy.

A knock on the door brought her head up.

"I poured you some champagne," Damon said.

That did sound lovely. Ruby checked the bubbles. They covered her nakedness.

"All right. Come in."

Damon entered with two glasses held in one hand and a bowl of strawberries in the other.

"Why are you doing all this?" Ruby asked.

He sat on a chair near the tub and put down the bowl and then one of the glasses of champagne. "I figured you haven't gotten enough of this in your life."

"Pampering?" She reached for the glass, careful not to disturb the concealing bubbles.

"Yes. And…you've had a rough night," he said.

She wondered if he had another reason. He was,

after all, in the bathroom with her while she reclined naked in the tub. He didn't seem to acknowledge that, though. He was being a gentleman.

It was true: she hadn't been treated like this in years. "I had a boyfriend right after high school who opened doors for me and brought me flowers," she said. Then laughed ruefully. "I should have hung on to him."

Then she would have never met Kid. She also would have never had Maya, and that was unthinkable.

"I'm glad you didn't." Damon moved to sit on the tiled edge of the tub.

At first Ruby was alarmed, but then the intimacy of him being there took over. She couldn't ward off the warmth he brought to her soul.

He lifted a strawberry. "I had one of these already," he said. "They're so sweet and juicy. It's what made me come in here."

"You wanted to share the experience?" she asked.

"Yes." He brought the berry to her mouth, and she took it and chewed. "Mmm." He was right. They were the perfect ripeness.

He ate one, too and handed her the glass of champagne. "There's a reason why people eat strawberries with their bubbly."

She sipped with him, unable to look away from his eyes.

After long seconds, he put down his glass. "I think I should join you."

She raised her brow. "What?"

"Yeah. You're getting the full effect of champagne and strawberries." He removed his shirt. "I feel left out."

She laughed despite the alarms going off in her head. He was being so fun-loving. And she couldn't deny temptation. She'd been fighting that even before she'd learned his true identity.

"Okay if I join you?" he asked.

"Yes." How could she refuse? She wanted him too much.

She bent her knees up and folded her arms around them while he dropped his pants.

And then all she could do was stare.

"What I should have done a long time ago." He climbed into the water and sat at the opposite end.

Ruby had gotten a good look at him. He was pleasantly endowed. She hadn't been with a lot of men and, other than statues and pictures, hadn't seen many naked men, but he was beautiful.

"Are you all right?" he asked.

"Uh..." She shook herself out of her stupor. "Yes. I think so."

"We're just taking a bath." He stretched his legs out on either side of her, knees bent to accommodate their length.

"Come here," he said, patting the bubble-topped water in front of him. Damon leaned forward, took her glass of champagne, and put it next to his and the bowl of strawberries.

"Just come here." He took her hands and pulled.

She slid in the water, and before she found her balance, he had her back against him.

"Okay," he said. "Now relax."

"Ha. Really?"

Damon picked up her glass and handed it to her. “Wait.”

She waited, hotness pooling low.

He presented a strawberry in front of her mouth.

Ruby took it and then sipped champagne, hearing him do the same behind her, feeling his muscles as he moved. She leaned her head back against him.

“No pressure, Ruby, okay?” Damon put another strawberry in front of her mouth. She took a bite.

He ate the rest of it and then sipped the last of his champagne.

She drained hers as well.

With both glasses on the tiles of the large, oval tub, Ruby waited in heated anticipation for what he would do next.

She was afraid to move. To think. To feel. To anything. Feeling wasn’t an option, she discovered. She felt powerful attraction for him.

He slid his hand around to her abdomen, setting her afire with the liquid caress. Then he lowered his face next to hers and nibbled her earlobe, his warm breath slow and steady and too, too arousing.

“Damon?” she was on thin planks that made up a bridge she could not cross safely.

“Shh,” he murmured against her ear. “I won’t do anything but this unless you want more. I won’t hurt you. Not ever.”

His words were like honey, warm and promising, but she had to be prudent. Smart. Cautious.

Didn’t she?

Damon’s hands ran over her body now, over her breasts, down to her abdomen and lower. A sound escaped her, a foreign sound. She had never made that sound with any other man. Damon pulled sexual hotness from her she had never felt before.

"Damon..." Ruby heard her breathless, lustful tone and tried to check herself. Her mind spun with uncontrollable feelings she could only describe as love, or the makings of it.

"Let go, Ruby." Damon kissed her temple and then her cheek, going down to the side of her mouth.

"Oh..." Ruby was losing control.

Or had she ever had that with him?

She turned her head to find his mouth. He met her, answered her, and she heard his satisfied groan.

"Damon..."

"Kiss me, Ruby..."

"Oh..." She did. She kissed him with all her heart.

Water sloshed. Her wet hand came up against his face, and his equally wet hand found her breast. She sought his tongue, and he gave it to her. They shared a tender play of loving intimacy.

After too many sensuously torturous moments of kissing, Damon ran his hands down her body, over her breasts and lower. He rubbed her. Ruby was taken aback by her instantaneous response. She had to break away from his passionate kiss to catch her breath.

"Damon..." If he didn't stop...

"It's okay," he murmured passionately.

The sound of his voice sent her tumbling over a sweet edge. She came so hard she cried out and arched her back involuntarily.

"Oh..." Ruby breathed deep several times. Then

reality descended. "That has never happened to me before."

Damon wrapped his arms around her. "Good. I like firsts with you."

Ruby relaxed against him. She hadn't had such an intense orgasm with any man, ever. She melted against him, her head resting on his shoulder, taking in the low, flickering light from the candles.

Damon's strong, muscular arm moved, and he filled their glasses. Then he picked up hers and put the rim to her mouth. She sipped, closing her eyes. She felt him take a drink from the same glass and put it down.

"I want more moments like this with you," he said.

So did she. But she didn't voice it. Something was missing. He had pleasured her and not received the same. Searching her heart, she realized she wanted him to feel what she had. She felt him against her lower back, an invitation he couldn't hide. He was hard as stone. She could have another orgasm. That would be new for her. Two in one day…

This was so intimate. They could easily take this all the way. But what would sex with him do to her mental state—and her emotional state? Deciding to ignore the warning in the back of her mind, she decided to let what might happen happen. She had already been intimate with him. What damage could be done by pleasuring him the way he had her? Besides, it touched her tremendously that he showed such restraint—and respect for her.

She tipped her head up to see him. His eyes were warm with desire, but in a contented way.

"Are you all right?" she asked.

He grunted a sexy laugh. "Never better."

"I bet you could be better," she said.

He sobered at that. "Ruby, you don't have to. I can't help what's going on down there."

Of course, she knew that. She also knew it was her body against him—her that was making him respond. Moving to turn to face him, she straddled him and sat on his hardness. Then she kissed him, just lightly and just once.

His smoldering eyes met hers. "What are you doing?"

"What I should have done a long time ago," she said, mimicking him.

He chuckled.

She kissed him again, this time lingering and deepening the caress. He put his hand to the back of her head, fingers going into her wet hair. She had her hands on his shoulders. The contact with his erection heated her up. She rubbed herself against him, making him groan a little.

Ending the kiss, she met his eyes again, lifting herself up. He helped her position his erection so that she could slide down onto him. Shards of tingly sensations rocketed through her. She could not have predicted he would feel so good. She tipped her head back and closed her eyes, then began to move, rocking her hips gently. The friction drove her wild.

Damon held her hips and lifted her, then let her down onto him. He did this a few times before she took up the same rhythm, grinding on him as she sank down.

The tingling intensified until she no longer felt a

part of herself. She was lifted into some other magnificent realm, where she came undone. Only then did she become aware that Damon had groaned and his breathing had quickened. He had reached his climax with her.

Ruby savored this moment with him. Nothing of their troubles interfered. It was only the two of them. She had never felt this cared for before. She dared not call it love.

Letting her head fall to his shoulder, she held on to the escape of being with Damon like this. But alas, earth came floating back. Then she looked at him. His eyes still lingered in what they had just shared. She sensed it had meant as much to him as it had to her.

Damon kissed her, soft and tender, packed with emotion. Ruby began to fret that maybe she'd gone too far. Maybe she should have at least waited.

More reality descended. The magic faded, and Ruby was left with the significance of this kind of lovemaking. He had deceived her for such a long time. Looking into his eyes, searching, she couldn't tell what he was thinking. Was he assessing her?

Disconcerted, she moved back from him. "The water is getting cold." Standing, she stepped out of the tub and retrieved a towel. He did the same.

Wrapped in the towel, she faced him. He grinned, clearly satisfied.

"This doesn't mean I trust you."

"Fair enough, but it's a good start." He grinned.

"It was just sex," she said.

"It felt like more than that, but we can go with that for now." He moved closer and kissed her again.

It carried with it a different sentiment, loving and not so passionate. Ruby felt connected to him deeper than ever now. Disconcerted, she stepped back.

"I'm going to get ready for bed."

"All right. I'll see you in my bedroom," he said.

She glanced back. "Do you think that's a good idea?"

"I do. How about you?"

"I'm not sure."

"Well, why don't we try it? If you get uncomfortable, you can go back to your room."

She might be able to do that. She'd decide after she had her nightgown on.

"Ruby?"

She stopped at the bathroom door.

"You do know you're safe with me, right?" he asked. "And I don't mean just from Santiago. I mean with me." He gestured with a nod toward the tub. "With that."

"I didn't. Thanks for saying something." He had relaxed her. He wouldn't push her when it came to love and sex. She could take some comfort in that.

Some. But not in totality.

Chapter 10

When Damon woke, his first awareness was that Ruby wasn't next to him. Why hadn't she stayed awhile to spend some time with him before getting up? He experienced a few seconds of regret before he realized what transpired last night had driven Ruby from his bed. Potent. Powerful. Almost incomprehensible. He'd felt it, and he knew Ruby had, too. That kind of love was as real as could be. Intangible. Rare. Beautiful. He was having a hard time dealing with that himself. The more he came awake, the heavier the impact became.

He had taken a big risk putting his heart out on a ledge. After spending months calculating his relationship with her, he had finally given in to instinct. Maybe it had all been worth it. If he could have a woman like Ruby for himself, he could have all he ever dreamed. He didn't have to pretend anymore.

However, the fact she'd left his bed spoke volumes. He hadn't expected her to do a one-eighty after their earth-shattering sexual encounter, but facing reality today didn't alleviate his disappointment.

He consoled himself by rationalizing last night happened because he had shed his barrier. Would he ever be rid of his distrust of women? He had taken things so slow with her, knowing the kind of man she had been with before and all she had gone through because of him, but he had also taken it slow because of his history, his experience with ultimate betrayal. And, of course, his investigation had taken precedence. He had allowed it to. From the moment he had first seen Ruby, something instinctual had gripped him. More than her beauty, something about her had filtered into him. Something sweet and innocent. He didn't like that thought. He trusted her as a person, but not with his heart. He didn't trust anyone with that. Not anymore.

But he still had an investigation to complete.

His plan was to make this as fun as possible for Maya. The less she knew about the reality, the better.

He showered, dressed and went out into the living area of his apartment. Ruby had her daughter planted in front of a bowl of healthy cereal and a Disney cartoon. Ruby had a cinnamon roll and a cup of coffee. Seeing him, she opened the oven and took out a tray of more cinnamon rolls.

Damon poured himself a coffee, feeling the tension emanating from her. He remained calm, but inside the stark reality that she could not face what had happened soured his stomach. He opened the refrigerator and took out an apple.

Taking a bite, he met her eyes. She watched him warily.

He took his apple and coffee to the table and sat.

She deposited a small paper plate with a warm cinnamon roll in front of him, then sipped her coffee and sat across from him, all the while avoiding eye contact.

"Are you all right?" Damon asked.

Her silent glance said no. And he should know no explanation was needed.

"Why did you get up before I woke up?" he asked, even though he already knew the answer. She was running the way his own instinct directed him to do. He would face it, though.

"We're going to take Maya to a festival. On the way there and on the way back, we're going to take her to places she may have seen piles of guns. We're going to make sure it's fun for her. Got it?"

"Got it." She smiled big.

She captivated him every time with that smile. Just by being herself, she lassoed him, despite any hesitation he might have. An invisible force kept him tied to her, his heart locked with hers. He would pursue her, but it might be the end of him.

Ruby sat in the passenger seat as Damon drove to the festival. She didn't say much, and neither did Damon, although he kept vigil of their surroundings and to ensure they were not being followed. He had taken a long route, so if anyone had tried to tail them, Damon had lost them. He made her feel so safe. Even as danger surely lurked, with him she felt protected.

That aside, Ruby knew Damon wasn't happy about

having sex and her reaction to it. She wasn't, either, and suspected they shared the same conundrum. Different causes but the same outcome. It had meant too much to both of them. While Ruby had been prepared for something good with him, she could not have imagined the extent of unbridled passion. That frightened her. Damon must also be troubled, with his history. Now they were left with what they had begun with, hardened hearts, distrust and disillusionment.

Maya hadn't caught on to the drama playing out between them. In the back seat of Damon's car, she had her favorite doll and cooed adorably while immersed in play. There was a time when Ruby feared her daughter might not ever find her innocence again, after all she'd witnessed with Kid. But here she was, a five-year-old in her own world, oblivious to evil. Ruby was so grateful.

"We're coming up on Kid's second warehouse," Damon said.

Ruby looked at the crumbling brick building that decades ago had been a factory of some sort. It had very few windows. She had never been inside, but she knew Kid would have secured some space in there so no one could access his loot.

Reaching back, she tapped Maya's ankle. Maya looked at her, and Ruby signed, *Do you remember this place?*

Maya looked out the window as they passed the warehouse, then shook her head.

Have you ever been here before? Ruby signed.

No. Why are we here?

It's on the way to the carnival. It's just an old, abandoned building. Part of history.

I like history.

Maya did like history, but in her young mind that was how Walt Disney had become an icon. She wanted to go to Disney World and see the castle. She also had become captivated by women who made a difference, like a famous supreme court judge people liked to celebrate. Ruby had to explain what a *pioneer* was. She had loved that. Ruby smiled as she continued to watch her daughter, who had resumed her play, completely oblivious to what the warehouse meant, much less its connection to Kid.

"Let's go to the carnival and then go by Mistress Number One's house," Damon said. "We need to make these trips fun." He kept his mouth turned away from Maya, lest she read his lips and start asking questions about what a *mistress* was.

He continued to amaze her. He was so in tune with Maya and her mental health. He understood what she must have gone through living with Kid, not to mention being found hiding at a murder scene.

Damon parked, and the sights and sounds of fun engulfed Ruby as she walked with an excited Maya toward the carnival. The Ferris wheel dominated the distant picture, the roller coaster second. All the other rides were in motion and produced squeals and laughter. The aroma of fried food wafted stronger as they reached the entrance. Sugar-coated food, too.

Damon walked faster and then turned to walk backward in front of Maya. "What do you want to do first?"

Roller coaster!

Maya didn't need a voice to let them know her excitement. Ruby would never get tired of her daughter showing such genuine childlike innocence. She searched and found a kiddie coaster, a caterpillar with a happy, grinning face. Smiling, feeling like a kid herself, Ruby pointed in answer to Damon.

He took Maya's hand and started toward the ride. Ruby took her other hand and had a feeling of family come over her, a feeling of rightness. She let it wash over her for now. Maya mattered more than anything, and she was gleefully happy.

They stood in line, Damon on constant lookout for signs of danger. Maya wouldn't notice or understand why, but Ruby did. She eyed him inquiringly.

"We're good," he said.

She smiled her appreciation. It was so nice to have a day like this, an escape from threats, albeit temporarily.

The line moved forward, and they finally took their seats in a caterpillar car, luckily accommodating three. Maya sat in the middle. The roller coaster moved slowly, up gentle hills and valleys and around a few brief turns. It was by no means a thrill ride for adults. But Maya loved it. Her laughter rang out, touching Ruby and making her share a look with Damon, who clearly enjoyed this as well.

Ruby tried to subdue the feeling of unity. The ride ended, and Maya reached up to take Damon's hand. Then she took hold of Ruby's. She smothered a flash of jealousy that Maya had taken his hand first. She supposed Maya's fascination and, yes, her fondness for Damon had much to do with her action. He hadn't been hanging around them that long, so the newness hadn't worn off. He had quickly become her friend.

They walked through the crowds until Maya spotted a train called the Looney Tooter. The cars were designed after cartoon characters like Tweety, the Road Runner and Bugs Bunny. Maya would love that ride. Sure enough, she tugged them forward, her little feet running.

Ruby laughed and saw Damon smiling. They got in line at a charming train station and boarded with cheerful, animated music. Maya chose the Sylvester car, and their journey began. The tracks wound their way around the entire carnival. Ruby took in all the happy people and the sounds and lights. Although beneath a bright blue sky, the carnival lit up. The train stopped, and Ruby found she didn't want this afternoon to end.

They rode the Tilt-A-Whirl and the carousel and two other rides before Ruby spotted a food truck that was sure to have delectable sweets. She led Damon and Maya there. As soon as Maya realized where they were headed, excitement made her almost skip her way over.

Funnel cake? Ruby signed.

Maya nodded enthusiastically.

She ordered that and two cotton-candy lemonade slushies for her and Damon. She'd share hers with Maya.

"I like a woman who orders for me," Damon said.

"I'm curious to know if you like it as much as I do," she said. They went to a table under a white canopy where several other people gathered to eat and drink.

Maya sat between them on a bench. Damon sipped the slushy.

Ruby sipped, too and watched him, Maya happily munching on her funnel cake.

After making much ado of taste-testing, Damon looked at her. "It's delicious. Yet one more thing we have in common."

What else did they have in common? He could sign. They had both been scarred by past relationships. They had both lost a parent when they were young. And they had similar tastes in food. Ice cream and slushies.

"A carnival experience isn't complete without a Ferris wheel ride," he said.

Finishing their treats, Ruby took Maya's hand and started walking through the crowd. Maya reached up for Damon's hand and he took it with a fond look down at her. Ruby would never get tired of seeing that.

They arrived at the Ferris wheel and got in the short line. Getting into the seat, Maya was again between them. Damon rested his arm along the back, his fingers brushing Ruby's shoulder. She looked over at him and shared a silent, intimate moment. Being like this was magical. Ruby had not felt more a part of a family unit since before her father died.

She imagined what it would be like to have a man like him with her and Maya always. He'd watch Maya grow up, grow out of toys and into a young lady. First dates. Prom. Graduation. Maybe he would adopt her and give her away at her wedding.

She had not had any of these thoughts before. She hadn't had time with Kid, nor had she had any inclination to imagine that with a monster like him. But now…

Now a warm, glowing cloud of loveliness blanketed

her. She could see them having these types of outings on a regular basis, as a family. The temptation to fall into this fantasy was too strong to resist, so she stayed there through the ride. She enjoyed the sights of the carnival below and downtown Chicago in the distance. She also enjoyed the feel of Damon's hand on her shoulder.

The ride ended too soon, and they exited their seats.

"Well, I suppose it's time to go," Ruby said, disappointed that their time together would come to an end.

"One more stop." Damon went to a shooting game where there were giant stuffed animals.

Delighted, Ruby watched as Maya, jumping up and down, pointed to the unicorn.

The game host was a skinny fiftysomething man with an untrimmed beard. He looked rode hard and put away wet. He didn't smile—well, he sort of smiled, a halfhearted, toothless curve to his mouth. His dull eyes said he had plenty of regrets, probably the biggest one being deciding to travel with a carnival and not put down any roots. That's how Ruby would feel if she were in his shoes.

Damon paid for a few shots and took aim. He effortlessly gained the top score and won the biggest prize. Maya squealed and still jumped up and down, more of a bounce.

Ruby laughed as the game host handed Damon the unicorn and he passed it down to Maya. It was so big she could barely carry it.

"What a grand finale," Ruby said as they headed for the parking lot. But as they neared the car, the magic of the afternoon began to deflate. Damon was a man who had expertly fooled her. He had known everything about her before she ever met him. All of his charm in getting to know her had been a ruse. How could she ever trust a man like him, a man whose job it was to live a lie?

Damon helped Ruby put Maya to bed, and the two of them went downstairs. They had gone by one of Kid's mistresses' house, and Maya didn't recognize it. They'd have another outing on another day.

He wasn't ready for bed yet, and he was sure Ruby wasn't, either. He could tell her mood had gradually dimmed as they'd driven to his apartment. He had fallen under the spell of enchantment, too. If he ever had a family, he'd make sure they did fun things like that together all the time. He had felt part of a family today. He couldn't think of anything more important in life than having that, a family. His job was extremely important to him, but that human connection trumped everything. He hadn't really considered that until now, how fulfilling being a part of a family could be.

Figuring Ruby needed to relax as much as he did, Damon took out a bottle of red wine and poured them each a moderate glass. He took them into the living room, where she was surfing channels with the remote. He sat next to her and handed her a glass.

With remote in hand, she looked up at him, hesitant at first, and then took the wine.

Noticing how she put all her attention into finding something to watch, he sensed her tension.

She settled on a history channel program about antiques. He liked her choice.

"I felt the same today," he said.

She scooted more toward the edge of the couch, sitting ramrod straight, and put the remote down.

"Being with you and Maya," he said. "It was so good."

Still, she looked straight ahead at the TV, without seeing it, he knew.

"It felt right, Ruby. Like being a family," he said. "I've never felt that way before."

Her foot bobbed up and down, an obvious sign of her discontent. Damon didn't relent. This was too important. They needed to talk about this, whether either of them wanted to or not.

"Can you deny it?" he asked.

Her foot stilled, and after several seconds, she looked at him, met his eyes. "No. But neither can I deny what a professional you are at your job. *Undercover man*."

He sighed and put down his glass. So much for trying to relax.

"I'm not sure I'm ready for this, either, Ruby, but we need to face what's happening," he said.

"What is happening, Damon? You're still in an active investigation. You're still playing a role. What am I to you? A vital part of solving your case? Of making your arrests?"

"You're more than part of my investigation. You weren't when this whole thing started, but you are now. You have to know that."

"That's the problem, Damon. This *whole thing* started with a great big giant lie. When I think about the possibility of being with you long-term, I wonder if I can ever trust you. Ten, twenty years from now, how will I ever know you're being honest with me? You could get tired of me and seek out something new, and I would never know because you are an expert liar."

"I'm not an expert. I play a role undercover because if I don't it could cost me my life. I am not an expert liar when it comes to real relationships. I didn't lie to you unless it would have put my life in danger. And I will never lie to you ever again. Now that you know about the investigation, there's no need for me to be secretive. I can tell you everything. You have no idea how much of a relief that is to me. I hated having to deceive you. I never felt good about that, especially when I became attracted to you on a personal level."

He watched her absorb his words and waver over trusting him, believing him.

"You could be lying to me right now. Your investigation isn't over. You need me to keep acting like I'm your doting girlfriend," she said. "You want us to have a fake relationship. I suppose that would be nothing new."

Damon scowled at that. There was no convincing her.

"We had sex, and today felt real to me," she went on. "I can't keep doing this, Damon. I think I should go stay with January and Sean for a while. This isn't good for me."

"No, Ruby. You need to stay here." Not only could he not protect her, her leaving would send the wrong message to Santiago. He didn't dare say that, though. She would assume he was putting the investigation ahead of her.

"Sean can protect me and Maya," she said.

"He has to work. He can't be around you all the time." He hoped she would see that reasoning.

She averted her head, clearly considering the consequences. Surely she wouldn't put Maya in that kind of danger. January, too.

At last, Ruby turned to him again. "I at least need a break. I'm getting worried about Maya's attachment to you more than to me."

"What kind of a break?" he asked. "Do you want to take a day to think things over? I'm not comfortable with you taking more time than that." He'd be worried sick about her and Maya.

"Maybe a couple of days. A weekend."

"Ruby, I really would rather you didn't."

"Why, so we can keep playing these roles? It's gone too far, Damon. I can't keep Maya in this situation."

Damon could see there would be no reasoning with her tonight. Their glorious day was too fresh, and their sex too amazing.

"Hopefully, it won't be for much longer," he said. "But even after this case is closed, I still want to keep seeing you."

"I don't know about that. Maya is getting way too attached to you. And… I am, too." She averted her eyes.

"Okay," he said. "Let's get this straight." When she looked at him, he said, "We both didn't mean for us to have sex."

"I agree," she said.

"I wanted to take things much slower, and I am pretty sure you did, too."

"I did."

"So let's get back to that. Let's be friends."

She half cocked her head, disbelieving. He didn't think they could be just friends, either. But he needed to reassure her.

"Okay, we'll cool things off for now," he said. "And I'll be careful with Maya. I don't want to rush into anything anymore than you do. I get you don't trust me, but if I'm being honest, I'd have to say I don't trust you, either. I don't trust any woman. It's part of my baggage from past experience."

She nodded. "I can go with that."

Damon caught sight of Maya tugging her mother's shirt. She signed, *Are you fighting?*

No.

It looks like you are.

We're having an adult talk, Ruby signed.

I like Damon. Don't take him away.

Ruby looked at Damon, clearly upset. He crouched before Maya. *Your mother and I are friends. We just have some grown-up issues we need to resolve. Everything is all right. Okay?*

Maya looked him directly in his eyes for a while and then gave a nod. *Okay.*

Damn, she was a smart kid. She was advanced well beyond her five years. And not only with intelligence. She had strong self-esteem and Damon would not be surprised if she went far in life. He didn't think that would be possible, however, without strong family bonds. Love.

Damon looked up at Ruby and saw her worrying

frown. Maya liked him, and she wasn't comfortable with that. He needed to convince her that leaving was not an option, even temporarily. But how would he do that?

Chapter 11

Ruby understood leaving was a risk, but she absolutely needed some time away from Damon. Moreover, she had to get Maya away from him. He had too much of an influence on her. She packed a duffel bag with everything she and her daughter would need for two nights at January and Sean's house. Sean was off duty, and they'd all be together. It felt safe. She hadn't told Damon. She had awakened Maya early and planned to leave before he woke. He'd only try to talk her out of this.

I don't want to leave, Mommy, Maya signed.

It's only for two nights. Don't you want to see January and Sean?

After her young mind contemplated that, she looked up and signed, *Yes*.

Ruby took her hand and glanced back to ensure Damon hadn't awakened. She didn't hear anything. Opening the upper door as quietly as she could, she took Maya into the stairway and, with equal quietness, closed the door. Going down the steps, she left the apartment and then the dark back room of the pub. The sun had yet to rise, so the outdoor lights were still on.

She kept looking back as she made her way to her car. There, she hurriedly unlocked it and opened the back door for Maya. After getting Maya buckled in the back seat, she put their duffel on the passenger side in the front and walked around to the driver's side. She stopped short when a man emerged into the reach of exterior lighting. She didn't recognize him. Average in height, he had dark sandy-brown hair and hazel eyes that held dominating confidence.

Before she could open the car door, he asked, "Where are you going?"

Fear raced through her, putting her on high alert. She glanced toward the back door of the pub. Had Damon awakened after all?

She faced the stranger, dredging up an outward appearance of courage. "Who are you?" He wasn't any of the men she had seen in the Foxhole.

"I'm someone Santiago calls when he needs to get his point across."

In other words, he was a hit man. Ruby grew frightened. She looked at Maya in the back seat. She was busy with a game on her tablet.

"Where are you going?" he asked again.

"None of your business. If you want to know, then

follow me." She hated saying that, but she was so sick of being bullied.

He became displeased, judging by the frown. "Santiago will be patient only for so long."

"I can't help you. I'm sorry." She faced her car door.

He took her arm and turned her back toward him.

Ruby yanked free, growing more alarmed. This was a man who knew Kid, a man no different than him.

"I'm not your enemy," he said. Then his eyes took a creepy tour down her body and back up to her face. "In fact, I'd like to be something of a champion to you."

"What?" What did he mean? How could anyone like him be a champion, much less think of himself as one?

"You are a remarkable woman, Ruby. You are stunning."

Ruby turned and opened her car door. "I can't help you."

"We aren't talking about that now," he said. "I'm trying to tell you I can make this situation easier on you."

Ruby felt like throwing up. Did he actually mean if she welcomed his attention he'd protect her?

"How do you propose to do that?" she asked.

"We haven't been properly introduced. I'm Carl Whitmore. It's a great pleasure to meet you, Ruby. Kid didn't know how lucky he was. But now that he's gone, maybe you and I could go out for dinner sometime, and I could tell you how I can help you. I'm close with Santiago."

So, he thought he could persuade Santiago to leave her alone—if she went out on dates with him.

"I'm not interested in dinner with you." Was he

crazy? She'd just been freed of Kid. What made him think she'd sign up for another horror show like that again?

"I'm hoping you'll change your mind. See, I can tell things aren't going well between you and Damon."

How could he tell? Just by her leaving in the wee hours of morning? "That's none of your business," Ruby said.

Movement at the back door of the pub drew her eyes there. Damon appeared and relief rushed through her.

The stranger looked there, and his expression changed from intimidating to angst-ridden. Clearly he didn't want this interruption. He must be one of the men Santiago assigned to watch her and Damon, except he had eyes for Ruby. Yuck.

Damon appeared beside her. "Carl. What brings you by?"

"I was just having a conversation with your girlfriend," he said. "If she's still your girlfriend. Looks like she's planning on being away awhile." He gestured toward the car behind her and Damon. "I saw her put in a bag."

"So what if she is?" Damon said. "What's it to you?"

"Santiago wants to know where she is at all times. You owe him something."

"It's time for you to leave," Damon said, stepping forward and towering over Carl, putting his body between him and Ruby.

No longer possessing that aura of dominating confidence, Carl looked up at him with a creepy but ego-challenged grin. "You can't escape Santiago."

"Santiago will get what he's looking for," Damon said. "I better not see you near Ruby again."

Carl sized Damon up and appeared to relent. He must be alone on his watch tonight and would be no match for Damon, who was much bigger and not afraid. Lifting his hands, he stepped back. As he did so, he looked past Damon, sending Ruby a chilling gaze, as if to say, *This isn't the last time you'll see me.*

With goose bumps spreading over her arms, Ruby watched him go.

"I guess we can expect to see him some more," Ruby said, voicing her thoughts aloud.

"Yeah. All the more reason to keep up appearances and stay close to the pub."

Damon wore a worried face, and Ruby had no doubt about the gravity of her situation. She had thought she should be afraid before, but to now have that confirmed gave her a sick feeling.

"Get Maya and come back inside, Ruby."

His commanding tone had a strange effect on her. Kid had been controlling, but Damon was not doing that. He was being protective. He was being a dad. A husband. A family man. And he was absolutely right. She could not leave.

Damon hadn't slept much the previous night. He was grateful Ruby had decided to stay with him, but she was a loose cannon. Her lack of trust sprinkled danger into his investigation and also for herself and Maya. No, he couldn't control her and didn't want to. He admired her spirit, her strength. He related to her reticence because he had experienced challenges in his life, too. He wished he could tell her this. If only she would believe him.

Yesterday they had spent the day avoiding each other. She played with Maya in the child's room for hours, until Damon had to go to work. He had thought of nothing else but her and Maya. Santiago and his men had not shown up last night. It had been quiet. Damon had been happy to be surrounded by normal people.

This morning, he made Maya strawberry French toast. Ruby hadn't awakened yet, and Maya had told him she was hungry. She sat at the table with her drawing book. He brought her a plate and put a cup of coffee down for himself, sitting across from her.

She looked up at him. *Why was Mommy going to take me to January and Sean's?*

They're her friends.

Maya picked up her fork and tried to pry apart a piece of French toast with her fork. Damon took her knife and fork and cut it into bites for her.

She stuffed a big bite into her mouth and happily chewed. Then after a while, putting down her fork, she eyed him. *Who was that man?*

Damon had to do some quick thinking. *He comes to the restaurant a lot.*

Mommy didn't like him, she signed.

"No," he said, signing as well.

Is he friends with my daddy?

He might have been.

Maya contemplated that before digging into her French toast again.

Just then, Ruby came out of her bedroom. She didn't look pleased with his early commandeering of her daughter's morning routine. He would not tell her it was Maya who had come into his bedroom and woken him. He had not gone to her mother.

He also wouldn't tell her about the earlier conversation he'd had with her daughter while he was making her breakfast.

Do you like kids?

"I love kids."

I can tell. Maya had smiled big, helping him mix the egg wash for the French toast. He had let her crack the eggs, picking out the broken shell pieces when she finished. He found the entire exercise beyond charming. He simply adored this kid.

Why don't you have any?

"I haven't been that lucky yet," he said, making sure she could see his mouth and ever impressed by her ability to understand him.

You have one now.

Damon had no idea how to respond to her declaration. He could vividly imagine living with her as a father figure. Ruby was the only question mark. Never in his life had he thought a child would touch him this way, a child that wasn't biologically his. Life sure was funny like that. Nobody could predict what lay ahead.

Ruby entered the kitchen, taking in Damon at the table with Maya.

"Strawberry French toast?" Ruby said sarcastically, eyebrow raised.

"With whipped cream," Damon said grinning at her expression.

I'm done. Can I go watch TV? Maya asked.

Sure, Ruby signed.

Maya went into the living room where she had dolls spread out on the coffee table and the television tuned to a cartoon.

Ruby got a cup of coffee and some orange juice and came to sit where Maya had vacated.

After sipping some coffee, she picked up Maya's fork and took a bite of strawberries and French toast.

Damon watched her. He was good at making that because it was one of his favorites.

She looked at him after she swallowed. "This is good." She stabbed her fork in the air above the plate.

"Thank you."

"I love strawberries," she said.

"Me, too."

When she looked at him again, he felt that now-familiar and fiery chemistry ignite. Just because they both liked strawberries. No, it went deeper than that. It was her body language that told him before she spoke that she liked what he had made, and it was their eyes meeting.

He reminded himself of his plan to keep his distance for a while. Not just for her comfort but for his as well. They were volatile together. Man and woman with live wires ready to spark.

Ruby turned on her tablet and read something. It looked like the news. Damon watched her do that and eat the rest of Maya's breakfast. Every movement captivated him. Her lips. The lashes of her eyes. The slope of her nose. Her soft, smooth and clear skin. She had on a sleeveless blue-and-white knit top that emphasized her breasts and light blue jeans that fit her butt perfectly.

"There's a kite festival this weekend," she said. "They have face painting."

Something fun for Maya while they searched for the cache of weapons. "All right." That reminded him of a time when his mother by choice, Nicole, had taken him and his brothers to a kite festival that had also had face painting and balloon decorating, among several sweet food trucks.

"I went to a kite festival when I was a kid," he said, wanting to share the memory. "They gave you kite kits where you could design your own. I made a really bad depiction of Captain America." He chuckled.

Ruby smiled with him.

"I collected Iron Man and Hulk and other comic figures. I had countless comic books."

"I was a typical Barbie-doll collector," Ruby said. "And I loved Scooby-Doo and *Big Hero 6*–type movies."

Damon chuckled again. "You had a taste for superheroes."

"Scooby?" Ruby laughed.

"He was a hero. He just didn't know it most of the time."

Ruby fell silent in thought, but her smile remained, albeit mild. "My dad was my superhero. Then he died, and that fantasy died with him."

Damon nodded. "Yeah, I know that feeling. After my mom died, things weren't golden. My dad was—and still is—a terrible role model. That's what really drove me to go into criminal justice. The kid in me never let the idea of superheroes go. I'm glad for that."

"Are you in touch with your dad at all?" she asked.

"Not unless I have to. I met with him to try and talk him out of going after the Colton will. He sometimes injects himself into my life and will likely continue to."

He saw her register how sad that seemed to her. "I have a bad dad, but I had a good family after my mom died."

"And now it's getting bigger," she said. "That party seemed to bring you closer to your new cousins."

He appreciated her noticing. "Yes. My dad and uncle are corrupted by my grandmother. None of us kids wants to see them take what isn't theirs. My grandfather took really good care of Carin and her twins. She's just bitter now and will do anything to get revenge. I'm not proud of that."

Ruby's eyes warmed, and she put her hand on his from across the table. "Of course you aren't. You aren't greedy. You're a good man, Damon." As soon as she said the last, her expression changed, and she withdrew her hand.

"I am a good man. I learned from the worst how not to be a bad one. I wish you trusted me about that, Ruby."

She resumed eating, not acknowledging him. Damon let it go. Eventually she had to start believing him. And if not, he had to find a way to let her go.

With Ruby engrossed in a remote-learning nursing course and Maya falling asleep on the couch, Damon went downstairs to work. He closed tonight. He was relieved Ruby and Maya would be right upstairs and he could keep a lookout for Santiago and his men.

He started his shift and worked for a few hours before Carl approached the bar.

"How does a bartender attract a woman like Ruby? She had Kid Mercer. He had tons of money. What do you have to offer?"

More than you, Damon wanted to say. "Kid took her daughter from her."

"Only because she wanted to leave him. He was teaching her a lesson. He would have taken her back once she came to reason."

Reason. Damon wanted to give this man a reason to go to the dentist.

"She's with me now," Damon said.

Carl laughed deep and sinisterly. "I doubt that."

Did this derelict honestly think he could win Ruby's heart just because she had been with Kid? Or did he think Ruby was available because he could sense the friction between her and Damon? None of these men knew Ruby, not beyond her name and her relationship with Kid. They only associated her with a drug-and-arms dealer.

Just then Ruby appeared before the bar. Damon became mesmerized by her. Such a dark beauty. She had changed into a sexy black sleeveless dress Damon wished she hadn't chosen to wear. What was she doing? Was she trying to make him lose his restraint?

She sat on a stool.

"You didn't tell me you were coming down here," he said.

Her glowing gaze was faked, but only he would know that. "I wanted to surprise you."

"You succeeded." Damon glanced at Carl, who observed their exchange in between licentious glances at Ruby's upper body.

Reaching for him, Ruby put her hand on Damon's. "I also wanted to apologize for arguing with you."

Damon fell completely out of his role. "You did?"

"Yes. I know you're dealing with a lot right now, and I haven't been much help. I want to change that." She glanced at Carl, who looked rapt. "If we find Kid's weapons, we stand to gain a lot, but it's more than that to me. You're more to me than that."

Wow. She was really pouring on the syrup.

"Okay. That's great, baby. I'm so glad you came down here to tell me that." He felt like nudging her or something. If she overacted, they'd be blown.

"You were ready to leave him earlier," Carl said.

She sent him a warning cat look. "We made up."

"Did you?" Carl brushed her long, thick dark hair back from her shoulder. "You don't strike me as the settling kind."

"Settling?"

"He's a bartender."

"And what are you?"

"I'm a businessman. I make a lot of money. I'm important."

Damon saw the flicker in Ruby's eyes. She did not like that response. Likely it reminded her of Kid. He waited for her explosion and whatever followed.

"What makes you think Damon can't make a lot of money?" she asked. "Damon is twice the man Kid was. You'd do well to recognize that." She tossed her head in the direction where Santiago sat, seeing, along with Damon, that he was watching their every move. "So would your boss."

Damon observed how Carl looked from her to Santiago.

"Ruby is off-limits to you," Damon said. "Or you can kiss your weapons goodbye."

Carl turned to him and leaned forward. "The weapons are ours. If you don't deliver, you have no future." He looked at Ruby. "But she might…with me."

Damon concentrated all his effort so as not to reach across and slam this putrid punk's head down onto the bar and knock him out. "Ruby is my girlfriend. Respect that or pay the price." He meant every word of that.

"Ooh, the man has some nerve," Carl said. "I saw that the other morning."

Although Carl acted bravely, Damon could see only Santiago's presence gave him power.

"It's time for you to go away," Ruby said. "I'm with Damon. No one else."

After looking at her several seconds, Carl gave a slight bow and walked away. He sat at Santiago's table and began talking to the group of men.

Damon couldn't wait to put him behind bars.

Unexpectedly, Ruby leaned forward and took hold of the collar of his shirt, pulling him toward her. Then she planted what felt like a heartfelt and passionate kiss on his mouth.

She knew Kid's men were watching. She did this on purpose. While he felt the full impact of her affection, it wasn't affection to her. It was a show. He didn't like that. He didn't like it at all.

* * *

Ruby heard Damon enter the apartment and lifted her head. She had fallen asleep on the couch, unable to fall sleep earlier. She was too bothered by having to play her role as his girlfriend.

She sat up as he approached.

"I didn't mean to wake you," he said.

"That's all right. I need to go to bed." She pushed the blanket off her and stood, facing him.

"Why did you do it?" he asked.

Hearing an edge in his tone, she said, "For Maya. Don't make the mistake of thinking I did it for you. I don't do fake relationships."

"Do me a favor and don't fake it anymore," he said.

She stepped back, surprised by the amount of emotion he exhibited. Had he felt it was real?

"I had to, Damon. They expect us to stay together. They think you can make me lead you to their weapons. If we aren't together, or they have a reason to believe we are drifting apart, then that puts us all in danger. I won't do that to Maya. She's been through enough."

"Yes. I've known that all along, Ruby. But that doesn't mean you need to make a spectacle. Only show me your affections when you really feel it."

Again, the amount of emotion took her aback. But he had been the one to deceive her, not the other way around.

"Oh, the way you showed me when I had no idea who you really were?" His betrayal still hurt. She could not deny that.

"That isn't fair."

"No? Why not?" She'd love to hear this.

"I didn't know you. I only knew what I'd read about you. Nothing could have prepared me for meeting you in person."

That was good. Really good. Ruby found herself fighting the urge to believe him 100 percent.

"Nothing could have prepared me for falling for you," he said.

Her defenses deflated, although she remained cautious. She would always have to remain cautious with him. If not for herself, then for Maya. She could not forget Maya. Her daughter came first.

"I'm sure it was exciting for you to fall for someone who didn't know who you were. You played a role. You fell for me. It was excitement and nothing more."

"No." He sounded emphatic. "It was more."

"What are you saying, Damon, that you fell in love with me? What, exactly, do you mean by 'falling for' me?"

She watched him swallow and stare into her eyes. His uncertainty was palpable, which only served to hurt her more.

"I fell for you, Ruby. I can't explain the depth of it. All I can say is you put me under a spell. I had no control over my feelings. I fell for you. I can't say it's love at this point, but I can say it swept me off my feet. This mysterious attraction I have for you. Everything about you. You're beautiful. You're principled, and you're a great mom."

Okay, that disarmed her. Was he being honest, or

did he intend to make her stop playing a role? She'd be more believable not pretending.

"I'm here until this is over and Maya is safe," she said.

He held her gaze for several seconds. "All right, then."

With that, he turned and walked to the hall toward his bedroom. She saw him pause at Maya's bedroom, checking on her before going to his room.

His concern touched her, reached beyond her barriers as many things about him did. She had to stay strong. She had to protect Maya.

Chapter 12

Maya didn't know that Ruby and Damon were taking her to Kid's club and a house he had owned before he met Ruby. Maya would most certainly recognize the club, and she might reveal a memory of seeing arms. Damon and Ruby might have missed some secret room.

Damon stopped across the street, looking around to make sure they weren't spotted. He had kept a careful vigil all the way here, ensuring their secrecy.

Ruby turned to see her daughter in the back seat, busy on her tablet with a game. She flapped her hand and said, "Maya?"

Maya stopped what she was doing and looked at her mother.

"Do you see that building?"

Maya turned toward where Ruby pointed. Then she looked at Ruby.

Yes. It's where Daddy did all of his bad stuff.

"Were the guns here, Maya?" Ruby asked.

No. Maya looked out the window and then back at her mother. *I don't want to go there. I want to leave.*

"All right, sweetheart. We're going to a tiny town. It's sort of like an outdoor museum."

A tiny town? Like dollhouses?

Yes.

Cool!

Ruby sat forward. "Let's take her by Kid's second house and then Tiny Town."

"Roger that."

Worried over Maya's aversion to Kid's club, Ruby rode in silence. Maya had made great progress in her therapy sessions, but reintroducing her to places that might have a negative impact on her could set her back. Ruby doubted Maya had any memory of Kid's second house, and going to Tiny Town would hopefully negate any bad memories that might creep up.

Ruby hated putting her daughter through this, but her main goal was to expunge Kid and his gang of thugs out of their lives forever. She looked over at Damon, undeniably grateful for his help and his affinity for Maya.

Damon caught her look as he stopped in front of Kid's house. He put his hand over hers.

"It's going to be all right," he said. "No matter what."

Meaning whether he and Ruby ended up together in a real relationship.

Warmth and love circled her soul.

Maya put her hand over theirs, and Ruby saw her big smile.

Family, she signed.

Ruby choked up and withdrew her hand. She signed, *Maya, do you remember this house?*

Maya looked and then shook her head.

"Let's go," Ruby said to Damon, disturbed and wanting more than anything for Maya to be able to live a normal life, away from all of this danger and these bad people.

Damon understood Ruby's discontent. Taking Maya to Tiny Town had been a great success. Maya had loved all the miniature buildings and the train. Even better, none of Santiago's men had tailed them.

Now he took them both to see his brothers and Nicole. He wouldn't have risked it if they had been followed. He was long overdue a family visit, and he sensed Ruby desperately needed to get a good dose of loving relatives. Maya, too.

Nicole had planned a barbecue at her house. She lived in a suburb of Bartlett. Damon had always loved her house. An old redbrick Victorian she'd taken from his uncle during the divorce. The wood floors creaked in places, and some of the rooms were small like they would have been way back when. The living areas had obviously been renovated and redesigned. The main room was spacious and full of coziness. And of course the kitchen did not remotely reflect the age of the house. Clean, bright and with top-of-the-line appliances, antiques sprinkled throughout to create an air of history.

The huge back patio was all light stone with a fire pit and seating both in the middle and under a metal gazebo. The yard was full of flowering plants and trees.

Maya took in the bright colors of the flowers, her tiny hand in Ruby's. They came in the grand entrance. This was familiar to Damon, but Ruby and Maya paused to take in the artistic mix of old and modern.

Something smelled great in the kitchen. Damon heard Nicole—his mother in every sense of the word—and Vita. Aaron, Nash and Uncle Rick sat in front of the television with a baseball game on.

All three glanced back and greeted them with a chorus of welcome. "Hey!"

"There he is!"

"Look who decided to show up!"

"Aaron, Nash, you remember Ruby," Damon said, hushing both brothers. They clearly weren't certain of the state of their relationship.

"Uncle Rick, this is Ruby, my girlfriend," Damon said.

Rick stood. He was in shape and had no shortage of personality and social fearlessness.

He came over to Ruby with such verve she took a step back.

"Nash and Aaron have told me about you," he said. "I'm so glad you see Damon for the good man he is."

Ruby looked at him unappreciatively.

Damon raised his hands. "I didn't tell them anything."

"January did," Nash said with a devilish grin. "She thinks another wedding is on the way."

"Come, come." Rick cupped Ruby's elbow and

took her closer to Nash and Aaron. "You haven't had a proper introduction to Damon's brothers."

Ruby resisted slightly, with another glance at Damon, as though she were being taken to a lion's den.

Damon smiled. "They don't bite."

"Aaron here used to box and now runs some successful gyms. We are all very proud of him. Nash here is an architect. Very artistic. Equally proud we are of him."

"Yes, I did hear a little about his brothers." She looked at Damon. "Before I knew he was an undercover DEA agent."

Rick patted her shoulder gently. "Forgive him for that. I meant it when I said he was a good man."

"In case you haven't noticed, our uncle is vivacious and friendly. His favorite pastime is spending time with family at gatherings exactly like this," Aaron said.

"I grew up in a big family," Rick said. "It stuck."

Ruby smiled, white teeth flashing and eyes twinkling. "That's enviable."

"Ruby has family in Wisconsin, and her mother lives here with her," Damon said.

"Ah, a Wisconsin girl," Rick said. "Fun *and* humble."

Ruby laughed again. "Not so much anymore."

Damon caught her gaze and hoped she knew not to talk about Kid here.

"You men seem more equipped to watch sports," she said. "I'm going to go see if I can help with the food."

"I'll introduce you and Maya," Damon said, and then to the others, "I'll be right back."

* * *

Ruby followed Damon into the kitchen, Maya's hand in hers. She entered into a glamorous cooking environment, bright and clean and uncluttered, splashed with color only an artist could pull off. Two women turned from the kitchen counter, their talking pausing as they faced the new arrivals.

"Mom." Damon went to a gently aging blue-eyed beauty wearing her dark blond hair up in sophisticated fashion. He hugged her with genuine love, and Ruby saw his mother's face over his shoulder, eyes closed with matching emotion.

Damon leaned back and turned to look at Ruby. "This is Ruby Duarte and her daughter Maya. Ruby, Nicole Colton." Nothing but proud devotion exuded from him.

She fell into hopeless attraction in this moment. Notwithstanding the obvious love, Damon said *Mom* so naturally Ruby was convinced he loved her as though she were his biological mother.

"Hello," Ruby said.

"Welcome, Ruby." She looked down at Maya. "Welcome, Maya."

Maya signed, *Hello.* Her daughter's face showed innocent fascination that bolstered Ruby's first impression of Nicole. The woman was full of heart.

Damon stepped back to include the other woman in the kitchen. "Never to diminish this woman's importance in my life, this is Vita Yates, Rick's wife and my aunt." Damon beamed.

Vita smiled at being announced as his aunt. Her light

brown bob framed her lovely face. She was slightly heavier than Nicole but not at all less genuine. Damon had told her about his quite extended family. Ruby was touched that he had received and still received so much love. This truly felt like a family. She didn't know what to do with how she felt, so bright and tingly inside.

"Would Maya like a cartoon? I see she has her drawing book," Nicole said. "Can she understand what's being said on TV?"

"I turn on closed captioning. She gets enough to enjoy it. Plus, I think she likes the actions and the colors more than anything." Ruby began to feel as though she fit right in. Maya, too.

"Amazing child, for sure," Vita said. "She's so young…and yet seems so advanced."

"I suppose she had to learn early. And I have to agree." Ruby looked down at Maya and signed as she spoke. "She is very amazing." Ruby ran her hand from the top of Maya's head down the back of her hair, feeling full of abounding love.

Maya's eyes softened with innocent love. Ruby thought her heart would burst. She asked her if she'd like to watch television. Being surrounded by a crowd of adults, she eagerly nodded.

Laughing, she and Ruby followed Nicole into a den off the living room and kitchen. It had pretty French doors and windows on the far wall and another wall made of a built-in bookshelf. Cozy and colorful seating surrounded the television above a gas fireplace. Nicole turned on the TV.

Maya took the remote and began surfing to her favorite channel.

I'll be in the kitchen, Ruby signed.

Maya nodded.

Ruby followed Nicole back into the kitchen and saw two other women had joined them.

"I wondered if you came with Aaron," Damon said. "Ruby, this is Fee. She's with Aaron now."

"Hi." Fee smiled, a striking blonde with a thin build.

Good looks abounded in the Colton line. "Hello."

"And this is my cousin Lila. We were all close growing up," Damon said.

"Hi," Lila said cheerily, her green eyes smiling and dark hair up in a twist. "Damon is like a brother to me, so you better not hurt him."

She said it with friendly teasing, but Ruby had a sense she probably meant it.

"Lila manages an art gallery in North Center," Damon said, clearly proud of her.

"I work with art, but I am the furthest thing from an artist," she said.

"You must know a lot about art," Ruby said.

"She does," Damon said.

"Damon is biased," Lila said. "But I do love it, yes."

Ruby smiled. "Everyone should be so lucky as to do what they love."

"That's Mom, too," Damon said. "She runs a catering business, so this barbecue is going to be delicious." He leaned over and planted a kiss on Ruby's cheek before withdrawing. "I'll leave you in these capable hands."

"I don't mean to be rude, but I'm going to join them in front of the TV," Lila said.

"We have enough help in here," Nicole said.

Ruby could only stare after Damon as he led his cousin into the living room. He had kissed her as though it had been a natural reflex, not rehearsed at all.

"Well, well, well," Nicole cooed. "It looks like Damon found himself a new girl."

"I wouldn't say that." Ruby didn't know how to describe her relationship to him.

"How did you meet him?" Vita asked.

Fee stirred the potato salad that Nicole and Vita must have just finished. There was a green salad in the making as well and a pan of baked beans that would go into the oven.

"Um...he came into the coffee shop where I work, and then...kept coming," she said.

"So you've been dating him?"

"We dated, yes."

Nicole looked confused. "Dated?"

"Um...we...sort of...live together."

Nicole's mouth dropped open, and she took Ruby into an exuberant hug.

Vita took hold of her next. "Welcome to the family!"

Whoa. That was a bit much for Ruby. She felt stiff all over. When Vita moved back, Ruby caught Fee looking at her with what she could only call understanding.

"You got a good man, Ruby. Just like I did, thanks to these fine women right here." Fee smiled.

"Yes," Vita said. "About getting a good man, that

is. All of us in this room know what it's like to be with one that isn't."

"That's an understatement," Fee said, widening her eyes cynically.

Ruby suddenly was full of questions, but she didn't want to pry. "I know you, Nicole, were married to Damon's father. He doesn't seem fond of him."

"Not many are fond of his brother, Axel, either," Vita said. "I was married to him. He was awful. Selfish. Mean."

"But then she met Rick," Nicole said. "Those two are inseparable. It's a wonder to see."

"I was married to a man I found out later was a drug dealer," Ruby said, leaving out the part where he kept Maya from her. "I thought I'd never escape him."

Fee appeared beside her. "I had a similar experience. My husband was abusive. I had to move and change my name…until I met Aaron. Now everything is fabulous. I never dreamed I'd be this happy. So don't give up on Damon. I know you probably have a hard time trusting men, but don't let go of a good one to save yourself agony in case it doesn't work out. Even if it doesn't, you'll be better than you were when you were with your previous partner."

Ruby looked from her to Vita to Nicole and back to Fee. She was among kindred spirits.

The doorbell rang, and seconds later Ruby heard Damon say, "What are you doing here?"

She turned to look over the island at two men who had entered, alarmed by the tone of the newcomer.

"Why are Erik and Axel here?" Vita asked.

Ruby turned to them. These men were Damon's father and uncle? She looked back at them. One wore a scowl, and the other seemed more aloof.

"I'm sure it has something to do with their mother," Nicole said. "And this can't be good, if so."

"Why are you boys mingling with those traitorous Coltons?" Axel demanded.

Apparently they had discovered their kids had gone to a party to meet their cousins. And oh, what a party it had been. Glamourous and fun at first, but for Ruby it had a bad aftertaste now. For the Colton cousins, it had been the beginning of a family alliance.

Damon and Nash stood at the door, and Rick remained on the couch, looking on. Aaron joined them, standing beside Nash. The three of them looked like brothers. Ruby didn't miss the body language along with the physical resemblances. They were close.

"Which one is Damon's father?" she asked Nicole quietly.

"The one who is grayer," she said.

Ruby saw they both had green eyes. They looked like brothers and not twins. Maybe it was Erik's grayer hair. Maybe it was his sterner look, but he looked older than Axel. Axel appeared less stressed out—and not as angry as Erik. In fact, Ruby wouldn't be surprised if his brother had dragged him here.

"Axel is probably here because Erik made him come," Vita said, sounding derisive.

Ruby said nothing, just marveled over their similar line of thought.

“How could you?” Erik asked, bitterness dripping from his tone and looking from Damon to Nash.

“How could we what?” Nash asked, more like a challenge.

“Betray your own father.”

Damon scoffed. “You’re no *father*.”

Erik subtly flinched, his head drawing back. Clearly he hadn’t expected his son to say something so hurtful. *Could a man like Erik Colton be hurt by anyone?* Ruby wondered.

She saw how Aaron observed the exchange, eyes hardening as Erik pretended he had been a real father to his half brothers.

“One party with those…those…impostors, and now you insult me like that?” Erik said, incensed.

“What you’re doing is wrong,” Damon said. “Those people are nice and full of integrity.”

Damon turned his back and walked into the living room. Erik followed, marching to get in front of Damon. Nash stayed near the entry, seeming reluctant to engage anymore.

Axel glanced at Nash and then went to stand before the television, near the couch where Rick still sat. He was more interested in that than his brother’s ranting.

Nash looked toward his father and brother, regarding Erik in distain.

“What we’re doing is taking what belongs to us.” Erik pointed his finger at Damon.

“Everything those Coltons have doesn’t belong to you,” Nash said.

He and Aaron walked closer to Erik and Damon.

"Grandmother started this," Aaron said. "You're only doing her bidding. All of this—" he swept his hand up and down Erik's body, indicating his demeanor and storming temper "—is to please *her.*"

"My mother is *right.* She deserved better from our father. She's only stepping up to defend us...and you, you ungrateful kids."

Damon shook his head, looking exasperated. "When are you going to wake up and realize she's been controlling you your entire life? You've been programmed to do whatever she wants, no matter how condemnable."

Erik stared at him, Aaron and Nash looking on, and Rick and Axel turning their heads to see Erik's reaction.

For a moment, Erik seemed stunned by the truth of what Damon said. But in a second, he reverted to his cantankerous self.

"You're all ganging up on me...and Axel."

Nash looked at Axel. "Uncle Axel?" he queried. "Are you in agreement with our dad?"

Aaron put his hands in his front pockets.

Axel looked from him to Aaron and then Damon, pausing there awhile before turning to his brother. "Yes."

So, he was under the grandmother's spell as well.

Ruby saw how neither Damon, Nash or Aaron were shocked by this declaration.

Some fathers didn't realize the impact they had on their families. Erik struck her as a man whose self-interests overruled any care or love he had for anyone around him. As long as people behaved according to his script, they were welcomed into his good graces. Disagree or go against his way of seeing things, and that made you an outcast, or at least subject to his wrath and contempt. Ruby had a friend from high school who grew up like that. She had watched the poor thing struggle to rise above damaging insecurities that wouldn't have been there had her father actually loved her for who she was and accepted her views regardless of how different they were from his.

Erik glanced around, satisfied that his brother had capitulated. "Where's Lila and Myles? Were they at that party, too?"

"Yes," Vita said.

Ruby became aware of her and Nicole on each side of her. Fee had taken a seat at the table, her feet up with ankles crossed on the adjacent chair, clearly entertained, albeit with cynical vibes.

"Yes, they were at the party," Damon said.

"What were you doing there? Turning your backs on your own family?" Erik asked.

"We wanted to meet them," Nash said.

"They're good people," Damon said. "You should talk Carin out of her lawsuit. It isn't right to do that to people who don't deserve it."

"Axel and I deserve an inheritance. Dean Colton was our father, too. What part of that isn't right to you?"

"You don't deserve the amount you're going for," Aaron said. "You weren't part of his life. You were part of Carin's. Stop her, Dad. Before it's too late."

Ruby could see there would be no reasoning with

him. She almost pitied him. How terrible it would be to live a life full of wanting and blame. Greed. Erik, as a product of his mother, depended on the handouts from others to feel important, superior even. Maybe he even deluded himself into believing he was envied.

"I'm not stopping anything." Erik looked at his sons one by one with disdain. "What a disappointment you turned out to be. You should be fighting for your family."

"Our cousins are our family," Aaron said.

Nicole stepped forward, going into the living room. "All right. Enough!" Her commanding tone spoke of all the turmoil she had suffered being married to a man like this. "It's time for you to leave. No one invited you here today, and you aren't welcome."

Erik leveled her a hard look. "These are my kids, too."

"Leave before we call the police," Vita said.

Rick stood when his wife said that, ready to protect her if necessary. He had been watching the exchange quietly up until then.

Axel glanced from his attention on the television to Vita. He surely must have been listening. Ruby didn't know what to think of him. He must agree with his brother, but for some reason he wasn't as aggressive. Maybe he wanted the inheritance but wasn't as confrontational as his twin. Maybe he preferred to leave the fighting to Erik. He just went along for the ride.

Axel walked to him. "Let's go."

Erik looked at him and then cast a belligerent gaze at each person in the room.

When Erik didn't move, Axel said, "Vita *will* call the cops."

"Now you talk?" Erik spat. "You never have my back."

"I figured you'd handle it," Axel said.

Erik glanced back at Vita, who put her hand on her hip and cocked her head, cell phone in her other hand, ready to call 911.

Erik muttered something Ruby couldn't hear, and he and his brother left.

Nicole shut and locked the door.

She faced the room. "Never a dull moment in a Colton house."

Everyone laughed.

Damon came over to Ruby and put his hands on her upper arms. "Sorry about that."

"Don't be. You told me he wasn't the congenial type."

He smiled softly, and she fell into the twinkling affection of his eyes.

"How are things going in there?" He gestured with his head toward the kitchen, where Vita and Nicole had returned. But Nicole watched them closely.

"Really great. I love your mom. Fee and I have a lot in common when it comes to men."

"Oh, yeah? What does that mean for me?"

"Maybe something good." She smiled in a way that felt flirty.

He chuckled, and before she could prepare herself, he leaned down and kissed her, not deeply, just a gentle peck.

Tingling everywhere, Ruby stepped back and

turned to walk to the kitchen, seeing Nicole smiling her approval. Ruby took up a knife and started helping to prepare the salad, glancing up at Damon every so often. How did he make her feel so loved? And why was it so difficult for her to accept it?

Chapter 13

Damon drove Ruby and Maya by two more places where Kid might have hidden weapons. They struck out again. Maya didn't show any sign of recognition. They even got out of the car and walked to give the child time to absorb sights, hoping something would trigger her memory.

The rest of the barbecue had gone smoothly—more than that. Damon could see Ruby warming to his family, and he loved it. He was afraid to believe she was also warming to him. She looked at him several times in a way that suggested her affinity to belonging to this—and him. But he was not one to make decisions based on instincts, good or bad. He followed them but didn't make life-altering changes just because they felt so damned good.

Now he had Ruby and Maya tucked safely away in his secure apartment, and he could go down to the bar to work. He crouched before Maya and told her he had to go to work and for her to mind her mother and have sweet dreams when she went to bed. Her eyes had taken on an innocent love, and she'd thrown her arms around his neck and kissed his cheek.

Damon was so touched he had kissed her cheek as well and said, "You are a precious little girl." He wanted to say *my precious little girl*.

It was true: Maya had found her way into his heart the moment he'd met her. Although he had known she was deaf, he hadn't been prepared for how smart she was for a five-year-old or how endearing. Then her personality had dug into him. Brave. Confident. Innocent. Even after living with the likes of Kid Mercer, she had overcome. Maybe it was her young age, but Damon preferred to think it was her strength that had gotten her through. Now she was like any other child her age. Except more special, as far as he was concerned.

Maya trotted off to the kitchen table, where she had her favorite coloring book.

When he stood up, he met Ruby's furious eyes. She wiggled her crooked finger for him to come out into the entryway, outside the door of the apartment.

"What the *hell* are you doing?" she hissed, hands on hips, mama bear wakened.

Damon took in her stance a bit longer and relented to honesty. "I love that kid, Ruby. I didn't plan on that. I didn't expect it. I've told you this before."

"My daughter is different. You can't mislead her!"

He raised his palms with two stop gestures and then lowered them to his sides. "I know. I am not misleading her. I truly adore her. More than that. She's…" He searched for the right words. "Special." No, that wasn't enough. "She's amazing…" No, that wasn't enough, either. "Ruby, she completely caught me off guard. I can't explain why she is so special to me. Maybe it's that she's deaf and doesn't let it get to her. Maybe it's how she likes me. I can't tell you. All I know…is I feel a powerful connection to her." He met her now-stunned look. "What that means for you and me, I don't care. I just hope I can keep being in her life. No matter how you feel about me."

Ruby continued to stare at him. And then she suddenly burst into tears and ran off into her bedroom, slamming the door.

Well, at least Maya wouldn't hear that.

Downcast and hoping he could pull off acting like a criminal bartender, Damon went downstairs and started his closing shift. It was early, so not many were filling the space, just the regulars who occupied barstools and likely sought to numb their pain.

He didn't take lightly Ruby's reaction to his and Maya's deepening bond. He was just as concerned about her as Ruby was. But Ruby would not believe that. Not yet. Frustration made him wipe the bar counter harder and more often than necessary.

The Foxhole owner eyed him every once in a while.

Damon checked himself. Ruby and Maya had to go on his cerebral shelf for a while.

An hour or so went by when Ruby appeared in front of him. She utterly surprised him until he rationalized she had waited for Maya to go to sleep and then had come down here to support his investigation. All premeditated, with the sole intent to protect her daughter. Or so she thought.

Damon would use this to his complete advantage—and not for his investigation. For her.

"Can I get you something to drink?" he asked.

"Ginger ale on the rocks."

Damon went to get her the requested drink, being sure to add an umbrella as a silent message. Flashy, just like their role-playing.

He put the glass before her.

"Thanks...lover."

He did not misinterpret her tone, although her expression revealed attraction. He wondered if at least that was real.

"Feeling restless tonight?" he asked.

"You stay away from Maya," she said in a low, growling voice. Mama bear again. She sipped through her straw with a hot look in her eyes. In the entire bar, no one but he would notice the extreme venom. She kept her face sexy, but her words and tone held completely different meaning. She didn't have four-inch, spiky-sharp teeth, but she sure could bite like she did.

Going to another customer, Damon was glad for the break so he could digest this extreme in Ruby. She'd do anything to protect her daughter. He got that. But her defenses spoke more from insecurity, threat. And Damon was a huge threat right now. To her and her alone. Her lack of trust was so deep he didn't think he'd ever be able to breach the barrier.

After a while he saw her glass of ginger ale was empty. "Another?" he asked.

"I think I'll have a beer. I can't leave too much of a teetotaling impression."

He brought her a light lager. "On the house." He glanced around, checking for signs of the gang.

Her eyes narrowed. Daggers flew at him. Ruby leaned back. "I know what you're doing."

"Tending bar?"

"You're playing your role. Showing Kid's gang members you're one of them," she said in a calm voice. She raised her hand casually, as though in conversation and not in anger.

"None of Kid's gang is here," he informed her.

"You stay away from Maya," she said, then took the beer and drank several swallows.

"No. I like her. A lot," he said.

Angrily, Ruby put the bottle onto the bar. She said nothing.

Just then, Damon saw Carl and the whole gang file into the pub.

He turned to Ruby. "Time for you to go upstairs."

She looked toward the door and saw what must be a souring reminder of all the pain Kid had caused her. Then she looked at him. "No. I think I'll have another drink, Mr. Jones." She finished her beer and handed him the bottle.

This was so out of character for her. It was worry over Maya and her attachment to Damon that fueled her anger. She was apprehensive about what this would lead to, and she must think it would lead to nothing, to him and her parting ways.

Oh, man. “No. Go upstairs.”

“I’m a paying customer. You don’t have to put it on the house. Give me another.”

“Ruby…”

“One more. Now. Or this all ends now.”

Meaning she’d blow his cover? Damon knew for sure she’d never do that. She was just mad that her daughter liked him.

“Okay.” Damon got another bottle of beer. Putting it on the bar in front of her, he leaned forward. “After this, you go upstairs.”

Ruby, with her elbows on the counter, leaned toward him like a drunken girlfriend, smiling sloppily and said, “Kiss me.”

“We don’t have to do that,” he said.

“Do it.”

At her commanding tone, he did.

He put his hand behind her head and brought her to him, kissing her firmly, unmistakably passionate. He did not have to fake it, and by the time the long kiss ended, he was certain she knew it.

He looked into her eyes, penetrating, telling her ruthlessly that she was treading on thin ice. He was the expert here, and there was no room for personal emotion.

Ruby leaned back on her stool and drank from the bottle.

He chuckled because Ruby rarely drank anything. “Will you be all right with Maya?”

“Yes. I’ll have tea when I go back up. And a movie. I’m not going to be able to sleep.”

"One thing I know for sure you are, Ruby, is a good mom."

Ruby nodded her thanks and took another swig.

Damon had to conceal his amusement before tending to other patrons. He kept an eye on Ruby, who remained seated, watching him. She'd go upstairs soon, but she must want to stay a bit to be around him.

Damon did not rely on his instincts when it came to women, but he would make sure nothing happened to her tonight. She would have a very mild buzz, enough to relax her and put her to sleep in pillowy slumber, but when he saw Carl approach, he went into kill mode.

He had to serve several customers and bar orders before he could go over to her and Carl.

"Carl was just telling me how beautiful I am and that he'd like to take me to dinner," Ruby said.

That was cheap. He turned to Carl. "Oh. That's charming. What did you say?"

"I said no." Ruby sounded like she'd deliberately slurred her words. "I need another beer."

Seeing her eyes, he knew what she meant. She played her role.

Damon got her another. She took a tiny sip and put the bottle down. She wasn't going to drink it all. She'd definitely had enough. She was probably feeling what she'd already had in a big way. Judging by her smile, he would say she was feeling pretty good right now.

Having to address his other customers again—the bar was filling up now—he left Ruby with Carl. He kept a close eye on her.

He could tell Carl was talking sweet gangster nothings to her and she was playing along, talking with him and smiling genuinely, or so it seemed. More like the beer had relaxed her enough to act.

He refreshed all his patrons and filled orders throughout the bar and then returned to Ruby and her ignorant suitor. The man clearly didn't know what he was dealing with. Tipsy or not, Ruby had unshakable principles.

"You are an amazing woman, Ruby," Carl said as Damon stopped at the bar.

"Yes, she most certainly is," Damon said. "She captured my heart the first time I ordered coffee."

Carl only then noticed him, or pretended to. He looked at him with displeasure.

"Santiago asked me to deliver you another message. You are taking too long to find what belongs to him. It's time to speed your progress along."

"We're working as fast as we can," Damon said.

"If Ruby knew where the stash was, you would have found it by now. The two of you appear to be close. Even…trusting. We've been watching you. So tell me…why have you not found it yet?"

"Ruby didn't know about the weapons, as I've told you. We're searching for them," Damon said. "We have some ideas on where Kid might have put them and are eliminating them one by one."

"Need I remind you that Santiago will be patient for only so much longer?"

"No. That message is loud and clear."

Ruby sighed like a satisfied cat. "I'm going up to the apartment." She stood from the stool with a gooey smile at Damon. "See you soon, darling."

"Can't wait," Damon answered, loving it.

* * *

Ruby stayed up with a book and a cup of tea. She had calmed down since going to confront Damon about his closeness with Maya. She was extremely worried about her daughter's well-being, but now that she'd had time to think, she realized she couldn't predict the future. Maya liked him, and he was a good influence on her. If they ended up parting ways, she'd be sad for a while, but she would bounce back. On the other hand, if Ruby and Damon ended up staying together, they'd continue as a family unit. Ruby admitted she feared that, and for good reason, but she couldn't live beneath that fear for the rest of her life.

She could, however, be discerning in her choice of men. Right now, it wouldn't be prudent to trust Damon completely.

Hearing someone coming up the stairs, she put her book down and twisted to see the door. The lock turned, and Damon appeared when he opened the door.

"Oh. You're still up," he said.

"Yes. I couldn't sleep." She held up her book.

He walked to the couch and sat. He seemed weighed down by something.

"Is everything all right?" she asked.

"I had a talk with Santiago again."

Ruby braced herself for more deadly threats over how long it was taking for her and Damon to track down the weapons.

"I asked him about your relationship with Kid," he said.

Why had he done that? He had trust issues the same as her. With both of them falling for each other, their hearts were on a chopping block with the knife getting ready to slam down.

"You did?" she asked.

"He told me one of Kid's men said Kid told you to leave because you had two affairs while you were with him."

Ruby scoffed. "And you believed him?"

"I didn't know what to believe," he said.

Imagining Damon having such a conversation with the likes of Santiago, Ruby came to two conclusions. "Okay, first of all, I didn't have any affairs, and secondly, Kid kept me from my daughter. Do you really think I wanted that?"

"Of course not, but he could have forced you to leave because of the affairs," Damon said.

"That would make sense if I had actually had affairs. Damon, I understand everything about fragile trust, but you're going to have to trust me on this one," she said.

He blinked, and she knew she had made headway.

"Besides, Santiago is probably trying to put a rift between us so that you'd be more likely to put pressure on me to find his weapons," Ruby said. "He wants you with me, but if you care too much about me, he loses control over you."

Damon blinked again.

Ruby scooted closer and put her hand on his cheek. "If I'd been in your shoes and someone told me something like that about you, I'd have reacted the same way."

Damon's eyes immediately softened, and he put his

hand over hers. "You're right about Santiago. He had to be lying."

Feeling a deeper connection begin to grow between them, she knew this was an important moment for them. They both didn't trust easily, but he had just trusted her.

Acting on impulse, without thinking, she lowered her hand and leaned closer, kissing him. He moved his hand to the back of her head, and she rested hers on his chest. This felt so good, she kept on kissing him. She let her doubts go.

She couldn't stop this. It felt too right, too strong.

His arm slipped around her back and drew her against him. She put her other hand behind his head and sank her fingers into his soft hair. Their breathing intensified. Her heart raced, and her entire body heated and tingled with love. She wanted him. So bad.

As she continued to bestow him with heartfelt kisses, no tongue involved, she sensed his waning restraint. Endless minutes passed before he took over. She loved how he did that. The man in him took charge of this sexual encounter. Seducer. Lover. Protector of the weak and innocent. Gentle soul.

She allowed him to be in charge for this spectacular kiss, but now she was ready for more. Withdrawing, she supported herself with her hands on his shoulders and straddled him.

"No, no," he murmured. "It's my turn." He held her and effortlessly placed her onto her back on the couch.

With her beneath him and his sexy gaze penetrating hers, Ruby gave in to pure desire.

"And this isn't going to be quick," he said.

"Good," she said breathlessly.

He kissed her much as she had him: soft, tender and full of love. Ruby tried to resist the powerful tide, but it was too strong. A tsunami of sensation. How he could do that with just a kiss she could not process.

Lying on the edge of the couch with his leg over both of hers, he ran his hand from her cheek down her neck and over her shoulder, before landing on her breast. He caressed a bit there and then progressed down to her waist, hip and then thigh. He just ran his hands along her body.

She raised her hands above her head and let him do as he pleased. After several moments of pleasuring, he kissed her, soft and slow as was the theme of this intimacy, it seemed.

Needing more, Ruby removed the *Drink Wisconsinbly* T-shirt she had on, seeing Damon's grin as she did so. He unclasped the front-fastening racerback bra, and her breasts sprang free.

She loved the way he took in the spectacle, taking his time, reveling. Then he unbuttoned his shirt and removed it. Letting him take the lead on this foreplay, Ruby kept her hands above her head. She watched him get up and strip them down. It was as though he understood she'd wait for him.

She would.

Naked, Damon returned to the couch, knees on either side of her. She watched him take in her pose, breathing long and slow and in passion. He moved so gracefully, powerfully.

Then he was on her, on top of her, flesh pressed to flesh. He had his elbows on each side of her. It felt so inexplicitly erotic. She would never be the kind to like being bound, but the surrender of giving him free access to her body numbed her mind to feel only ecstasy. It was *pure* ecstasy. For this night, she could give absolute trust. She realized just then, it was his trust that made her do this, to let go this way.

Ruby lifted her leg and draped it on the back of the couch, giving him room to lie between her legs. She felt his hardness against the place that craved him, but he didn't rush. He kissed her reverently. She matched it, effortlessly she realized. They danced in love.

Unable to resist any longer, Ruby brought her hands to his skin. She touched his shoulders, his biceps, the sides of his powerful torso, down to his rear and back up again, resting on his firm, smooth, muscular back.

Damon lifted his head, and she met his eyes. Beautiful, manly eyes so full of passion.

He positioned his erection at her opening and began pressing in. She was so wet it didn't take much effort. He slid right in.

Ruby dug the back of her head into the couch and spread her knees wider.

"Damon." His name came unbidden from her.

"Yes," he answered gruffly.

He began sliding in and drawing out just a bit, angling to brush her clitoris every other stroke. It was enough to bring her to a state of utter mindlessness. Nothing else existed but him and what he made her feel. She came too quickly.

But he came with her. As Ruby's world melted back down to reality, the thought dawned on her that no other man would ever match her like this one.

Chapter 14

Watching Ruby spread peanut butter and jelly over a toasted muffin with mechanical movements, Damon recognized her mood. Ever since waking with her—yes, they slept in his bed—she sometimes had a dreamy look and less frequently a troubled one. Right now she appeared entranced, absorbed in thought. He hoped those thoughts were in the clouds and full of future imaginations. His certainly were.

After last night, he'd officially thrown in the towel. Ruby was what he wanted and needed in his life. And not just her. Maya, too. He feared what Ruby could do to him if she ran from her own insecurities and sought safer, loveless ground. But he was filled with a new and invigorating certainty he could no longer deny.

He kept this to himself. Ruby would not be able to

handle such a declaration right now. He had to end this case and then concentrate on convincing her this was meant to be. Him. Her. Maya. A family. A real one. His heart soared just thinking about it.

A tug on his shirt brought his attention down to an adorable dark-haired five-year-old.

You're burning the eggs.

Damon looked at the pan of eggs he'd been working on and was startled to see he was, indeed, burning the eggs. Ruby's mechanical spreading of peanut butter came back and slapped him. They were both in some sort of trance.

Damon removed the eggs from the burner. Ruby had stopped moving her knife and looked at him, then the pan, then at Maya.

"Maya is an observant soul." Damon made sure she could see his lips but also signed.

She beamed a big smile and climbed up onto an island stool.

He washed out the pan and started over with fresh eggs, ever aware of Maya.

Ruby prepared a bowl of cubed cantaloupe, eyeing Damon and Maya, whose eyes were all for him. Ruby clearly did not like that.

Damon pretended not to notice. He finished the eggs and put together Maya's plate. Then he prepared his and Ruby's, ever aware of Ruby so close to him, their arms or shoulders brushing every once in a while.

Ruby sat on one side of Maya and he on the other at the island. This was all impromptu.

Maya was well into her meal by the time he and Ruby dug in. Damon noticed her glance at him often.

She did that a lot. Watched. Being deaf, she must have amazing abilities to read people from only their body language.

After a time, breakfast approached an end as hunger waned. Ruby put her fork down and sipped some orange juice. She leaned back against the stool and watched her daughter for a time. Damon would never get tired of that, the vision of a mother like Ruby just watching her daughter.

"I had a thought today," Ruby said.

Maya had stopped eating and now drew in her notebook.

This seemed important to Ruby. She had clearly waited for Maya to be fed and preoccupied to bring this up. Plus, her demeanor was completely different. Whatever she had to say would carry big weight.

"Kid had another house in Chicago," she said. "Maybe he brought Maya there…without me."

Ruby stood and took her plate to the sink, beginning to clean up.

Seeing her distress, Damon went to her. He stood behind her and put his hand on her shoulder. "None of this is your fault, Ruby. This is Kid's doing. He made some bad choices in life, for whatever reason. You were sucked into his vortex. Deceitful vortex."

"That doesn't make it any easier," she said.

"I know. I'm going to be your champion, Ruby. I will expunge that man from your mind, and I will be the man you deserve," Damon said, meaning every word.

She faced him and met his eyes. "You mean that? You're being honest?"

"Yes."

He watched her struggle to believe that. He suppressed a grin. She had been that way since he'd first met her: reluctant, guarded. He had never had to work this hard for a woman's affection before, and he discovered he not only loved it, but he also had tremendous respect for Ruby. Her penchant for surety would also secure his. Except...he was already sure. He'd stop at nothing to win her trust.

He kissed the tip of her nose. "We'll go by there tomorrow, then we'll take Maya to the zoo. If she gets any negative vibes, that should take care of her."

Ruby turned, putting her hand over his on her shoulder. "You're an amazing man, Damon Colton."

He breathed a chuckle. "I'm just catching the bad guys."

"I just hope I'm enough for you."

"You are, Ruby. The only question is...am I enough for you?"

Damon's words kept running through Ruby's mind as they drove toward Kid's old house. *Am I enough for you?*

She knew exactly what he meant. He didn't mean to question whether he, personally, was enough for her. He was. He meant was he enough for her to trust?

Damon pulled up to the house where Kid had stayed on occasion. He parked across the street.

"Maya." Ruby reached into the back seat and waved to get her attention.

Maya looked up from her coloring book.

Ruby signed, *Have you seen this house before?* Ruby pointed.

Looking out the window, Maya nodded.

Did you see any guns in there?

Maya shook her head, and Ruby let out a disappointed breath. She glanced at Damon. "I can't think of any other places where Kid would have taken her."

His expression became as grim as she felt.

"What now?" Ruby asked. Santiago would surely come after them. He'd want them dead if they came up empty-handed.

Then from the back seat, Maya poked Ruby's shoulder.

She looked back and saw Maya stretch her arm out and point to the house next to the one Kid had owned.

A surge of hope ran through Ruby. The house appeared as though it had been left unmaintained for quite some time. Years. It was in poor condition. This was an older subdivision, and the houses much smaller than the one she and Kid had lived in. But Kid had found the charm irresistible and purchased a house here.

Damon took out his phone and called someone. "Yeah. Colton here. I think we found them."

He must be talking to his boss or some other member of his undercover team. He gave the address and said it was an abandoned house. At some point he must have informed them that Maya had drawn pictures.

"I'll wait to hear from you," Damon said.

Then he turned to Ruby. "They're going to find out what happened to the owner or their family. If the owner intentionally left with no plans to return or the family just doesn't care, I can go in without a warrant."

Ruby sat with him in silence while they waited. Who knew how long it would take?

"How many people are working your case with you?" she asked.

"Quite a few. There's administratives, other agents, special-forces types. Not all of them know the details of my cover, for obvious reasons, but they are all ready for a raid. I report to the agent in charge."

They were all waiting for an end to this investigation. Just like her. Except Ruby wasn't law enforcement, and her stake in this was personal.

"This reminds me of my grandmother's house. In a way." He took in the other houses, many like the one his estranged and dead grandfather had bought for her.

"How so?" Ruby asked.

"It was a Federal-style mansion built in the 1800s."

"These aren't mansions," Ruby said. "That's probably why Kid didn't come here much. He had fantasies of riches he'd never be able to possess."

Damon could see that. People who gambled their lives on drugs and violence usually wound up dead or in prison. Not many made it as far as El Chapo.

He rested his head back, content to wait for his team to dig up information on the abandoned house and to spend the time with Ruby.

"What's your grandmother's house like?" Ruby asked.

He rolled his head to see her. She had leaned back as he had. He smiled gently. They were two peas in a pod.

Rolling his head straight again, he said, "Old. Too big for her to manage." He took a mental tour through the home. "Even the furniture is old. Most of it belonged to the previous owner."

"Sounds nice to me," she said.

"Grandmother can't afford the upkeep on a place like that. Most of it is boarded up. She needs money to fix it up. That's one reason she's going for the aorta to get our cousins' money."

Ruby turned her head to look out the passenger window. He could see she was in thought.

"It's kind of sad your grandmother is that way," she finally said, turning back to look out the windshield. She sighed slowly, relaxed. "There is so much more to life… Family… Love."

That made him sigh the same way. "Yeah."

Their moment was rudely interrupted by his phone going off. He answered. It was his team.

"What does the exterior look like?" the agent asked.

"Basement windows are boarded up. Weeds everywhere. Paint chipping. Second-story windows are also boarded."

"We couldn't get a hold of the owner. Go in and see what's inside. If it appears abandoned, do the search. Call if you need backup."

"Roger." Damon lowered his phone and looked at her. "I'm going in. You wait here with Maya."

Ruby readily agreed. Maya was now absorbed in her book. She was a voracious reader. Watching Damon disappear around the back of the house, she tried to stave off a wave of worry. What if someone was in that house?

* * *

Damon peered into several windows and saw the house wasn't furnished and was in grave disrepair. When he opened the single screen door, it fell off its rusting hinges. Leaning it against the house, he tried the doorknob. It didn't budge. The handle looked new, probably the only new thing on the property in decades. To Damon, this was a good sign. Kid would have thought to secure his stash.

Seeing the kitchen window was cracked, he used a rock to break the glass. Clearing the shards, he crawled through. Dirt and broken cabinets greeted him. It smelled moldy. He walked through the rooms, looking out the front window to check on Ruby and Maya. Ruby looked toward the house, and Maya entertained herself in the back seat.

He checked every closet and searched for secret doors. The second level was empty and filthy like the first. Damon hadn't expected to find much up here. He headed down to the main level and went to the basement stairs. The door was padlocked. A sure sign something valuable was down there. Damon left it untouched. The weapons had to be here.

He returned to the car, on the way telling his team to move in. He didn't want to risk being here longer than necessary, lest he alert Santiago and blow his cover.

Time to go to the zoo.

Maya sat next to the giant giraffe Damon had bought for her yesterday. Morning now, Ruby prepared cheesy scrambled eggs, toast and fruit for breakfast. Damon sat at the table working on his laptop. He'd been on the phone for hours last night. The DEA had found Kid's stash of weapons and ammo in the basement of the abandoned house.

Ruby shied at believing her nightmare would finally be over. Even in death, Kid could still haunt her.

She brought plates to the table, then went to get Maya's attention. She left her morning cartoon, awkwardly and adorably carrying the giraffe. She put the stuffed animal on the chair beside her.

Ruby took the seat adjacent. Having placed a plate next to Damon's computer, she waited for him to pry himself away from work and notice.

He grinned. "Sorry."

She felt his excitement. It matched her own.

They began eating, Maya taking intermissions to have a signing conversation with Giraffe.

Ruby enjoyed the peaceful moments while they shared a meal as a family. She was ever curious to know what resulted from all his work so far today.

"So…what are you going to do with Santiago and the guns?" she asked.

Maya was busy eating and carrying on with her giraffe.

"I'm going to use the weapons to coerce him into a deal. I'll demand money for them. It'll be a sting. If he goes for it, we'll arrange to meet at the abandoned house, make the deal and carry out the raid."

Ruby worried at that. "But Santiago thinks he's in charge of you. You're like…his boy."

Damon chuckled. "I am not his boy. I have the weapons. He doesn't know where they are. All he expected from me was to find them. He didn't anticipate

I'd use them against him. I made sure of that. His greed and power-hungry ego will be his downfall."

That had been his plan all along. Make Santiago believe he was acting to protect Ruby and Maya, that his main goal was to be accepted into the criminal organization, to make money. He had done that. Santiago had no idea who he was dealing with. More than an undercover agent, Damon was no man's man.

Chapter 15

Although Damon didn't like taking Ruby with him to meet Santiago, for the sake of the investigation her appearance would be best. After all, Santiago believed she was the one who had led him to the weapons and ammo. They had dropped Maya off at January and Sean's home. Damon would take Ruby there before he and his task force met Santiago at the vacant house. Santiago wouldn't want to wait.

Damon spotted Santiago sitting at his claimed table with Carl and Orlando, two of his most dangerous men.

He pulled a chair out for Ruby and she sat, looking sexy in a white summer dress. He sat beside her.

"I assume there is a reason for this urgent meeting," Santiago said. "Why not just tell me over the phone?"

"We found the guns and ammo," Damon said.

Santiago's eyes moved to Ruby. "You finally gave in and told him?"

"I didn't know where they were. I only knew where Kid would have gone. It was a process of elimination," she said.

Now Santiago looked pleased. "Very good. Very good. Where are they? We need to arrange shipment to one of my warehouses."

Damon remained calm, meeting Santiago's eyes intently. "It's not going to be that simple, Santiago."

Santiago's brow rose. "Oh?"

Carl and Orlando glanced at each other, then watched Santiago for signs of whatever order he might decide to pass on to them. Damon always marveled over the psychology that drove criminals like them. They were pawns. They took orders. They lived in threat of being killed. And for what? He doubted even they knew the truth of that. They grew up in volatile homes with little or no love. They learned crime and lived crime.

"We want a finder's fee," Damon said to Santiago.

"You want money." He said it flatly, glaring at Ruby as though blaming her for this.

"Those guns and ammo don't belong to you. Not yet. They belonged to Kid Mercer. The way I see it, whoever find them gets them. Now, I'm a generous man. I can be reasonable. I think ten percent of their value should do it."

"You've got balls demanding that," Santiago said. "I took over in Kid's place. Anything that belonged to him now belongs to me."

"That's why I called it a finder's fee. You've been

on me to give them to you, now I can, but you have to pay for all my effort."

Santiago half stood and pounded his hand on the table. "How dare you?"

Ruby flinched and stood, backing away from the table. Orlando drew his gun.

"You will give me every one of those guns and the ammunition. I want them tonight. If you don't bring them to me, I'll have you killed." He looked at Orlando, who nodded once.

Damon stood and took Ruby's hand to reassure her. He was accustomed to dealing with characters like this; she wasn't.

"You don't seem to understand," Damon said. "I have your weapons. I know where they are. If you want them, you'll pay me my finder's fee."

"Your finder's fee." Santiago looked at Ruby.

"Ruby has nothing to do with this deal. This is my deal." Damon leaned over the table, his palms supporting him, bringing his face inches from Santiago's. "Give me the address for your warehouse. I'll bring the guns and ammo. When you pay me ten percent of their value, I'll give them to you."

Santiago met his eyes hard for a while before cynicism took over. "You surprise me, Mr. Jones. I had you pegged for another follower. But here I discover you are more than that."

"I am much more than that. I can make you a lot of money if you give me a chance."

"I thought that's what I did when I gave you the opportunity to find and hand over my weapons."

"Which I have done. I found your weapons. Now I expect to be paid for that service," Damon said.

After a moment, Santiago's expression changed from dangerous to grinning evilly. "I like your style, Mr. Jones. I always have."

"Santiago," Orlando said in a warning tone.

Santiago lifted his palm to silence him. "No. I'll give you this deal. Ten percent." He turned to Carl. "Get everyone ready." Then he faced Damon. "The alley behind Kid's nightclub. Midnight tonight."

That would be difficult to orchestrate with his team. "I'll be there."

Ruby was extremely worried. Damon dropped her off at January and Sean's, kissed her quickly and said he'd call when it was over. Now her imagination ran wild. She had no illusion as to the kind of men he was up against. Kid had been ruthless in his doling out punishments when his men didn't rise to his ridiculous expectations. Santiago was every bit the tyrant Kid had been.

Sitting on the back patio with January drinking iced tea, Ruby was glad Maya wanted to color. She was too distracted by her thoughts.

"He knows what he's doing, Ruby," January said.

Ruby looked at her, realizing her worry was transparent. "I know. It's just… I was with Kid long enough to know what they're capable of."

"Damon is a DEA agent. He's in law enforcement, like Sean. They are good at what they do. You just have to trust him."

"Huh. Trust." Now there was a word.

January laughed lightly. "It's always hard going into a new relationship. You never know which way it's going to go."

Ruby appreciated her candor. "Yes, and both Damon and I have been through rough past relationships. His role-playing while he was undercover didn't help. I admit I'm overly cautious and maybe a little paranoid, but I can't help it. It's just…ingrained in me based on experience." Horrible experience.

"You'll be fine. Once all the turmoil is over, it'll just be you and him."

That would be nice. Ruby wasn't sure it was that simple, though. "Maya has grown close to him."

"That's great! She needs an influence like Damon in her life. He's a hero, not a criminal. I think he'd make an awesome dad. I mean, I can't say I know him well yet, but he seems like an honorable man."

"He is," Ruby had to say. It was the truth. "Every time I meet someone new, I try to tell myself not to have any expectations, but I want to. I want to believe I can have a life with someone like Damon, but I'm so afraid to let go."

"Everyone is. Just give it time. It'll all work out in the end."

Ruby liked January's optimism, but she had already gone through the trials with Sean. They were a solid couple now. Ruby could not say that about her and Damon.

"I can tell you love him," January said.

Did she love Damon? Thinking about the man in that context, she got all warm and tingly inside.

"And I saw the way he looked at you at the party. He's a goner. He's fallen for you hard."

Ruby laughed, full of joy, unbidden and without prior thought. Natural. She caught her breath. No. Damon had the power to break her heart like no other. And Maya's.

She turned her gaze away from January and found herself looking out at trees and flowers. It didn't soothe her. Damon might very well not survive what he was about to attempt. He had told her before he dropped her off that it would be best if she came with him to make the deal. She was an integral part of the investigation. But Ruby had thought only of Maya and resisted. Damon, being the man he was, hadn't pushed her.

"Ruby?" January said.

Ruby sprang up. "I have to go. Will you watch Maya?"

"What are you doing?" January stood.

Sean had gone out to get dinner, so he wouldn't get in her way. "I have to go to him."

"No, Ruby. It's too dangerous."

"January, please. I know Kid and his gang. They'll be suspicious if I'm not there. I *have* to go. Now."

January met her eyes, and Ruby saw her understanding. She related to what it was like to be with men who weren't afraid of confronting bad people. She had a protective nature like Ruby.

"Okay," she said. "Maya is safe here."

Ruby threw her arms around her and breathed a thank-you.

"Just come back alive, all right?"

"I will. Nothing will keep me from my daughter."

As she hurried from the house, Ruby wondered if this situation might be the one to keep her from her daughter—if she didn't survive the night.

But she could not stand by and do nothing. Damon was in law enforcement, but Ruby knew way more than him about the evil that surrounded Kid.

Standing in the back of a conference room, Damon listened to his boss lay out the strategy of the raid. They'd already gone through the drill, but this was a refresher and also a pep talk, a strength-booster. They had the element of surprise. Santiago had no clue what was coming. The task force had the advantage, but they could not underestimate the enemy.

"One more time," Brian McNatt said. Special agent in charge of the Chicago Field Division of the US Drug Enforcement Administration, he had a commanding presence. "Somebody tell me the plan."

The DEA had partnered with federal, state and local law-enforcement agencies to bring down Kid Mercer's reign of terror.

"We loaded the weapons into a truck and are ready to meet Santiago at the nightclub," Damon said. "We'll have snipers in position and a team surrounding the alley, some inside buildings, some out of sight outside. There are more agents in vehicles who will sweep in once the exchange of money happens."

"And you're certain Santiago and his men aren't aware of your identity?" the agent asked.

"I'm certain." Thanks to Ruby for helping him with that. Kid's gang of thugs would not expect the DEA descending on them. Damon would relish every moment, even as dangerous as this move would be.

"What about Duarte? Why isn't she here?" Brian asked.

Damon ground his teeth, He needed her with him to make this go smoothly. He hadn't forced her, though. He had gotten her into this mess. He didn't want to put her through any more stress.

"She's somewhere safe," he said.

"You didn't tell her to be here?"

"No, sir."

Brian studied him a while. "I understand. You have to be extra careful without her. She was Kid's girlfriend, the mother of his child. She's the reason we found the weapons."

"I'm aware of that."

The room was silent as the gravity of the situation sank in.

"All right." Brian checked the time. "Let's get this done."

Before anyone could move, the sound of running feet and the door to the big conference room bursting open stopped everyone. Damon turned to look and saw Ruby, breathing fast in her rush to get there.

Damon's heart swelled with love. She had come to help him.

He stood as she walked hurriedly to him and threw her arms around him. Conscious of the crowd of burly agents surrounding them, he held her through the brief hug.

Then she leaned back. "I had to come here. You need me. You all do."

He grinned. Not caring who saw, he kissed her. Cat calls erupted along with clapping.

"My brave woman," he said when the kiss ended. "Let's go crush Kid's gang."

Yeah, and then start a new life together. Damon didn't say that now, but he felt sure of the course ahead of him. He just had to convince her she had the same one. With him.

Ruby and Damon arrived at the meeting place. She saw Santiago with his entourage of armed men. Carl, Orlando and Sonny flanked him, each carrying mean-looking automatic weapons. Her heart raced. This could go so bad in such a short amount of time. She looked over at Damon.

He winked at her.

She smiled. He was totally in his element. A flood of trust and love suffused her. She had never felt anything like it before.

He would get them through this.

She got out of the car and walked with him toward Santiago.

"Where are my guns?" Santiago asked.

"Parked not far from here," Damon answered.

"You have someone else involved? Who is with them now?" he demanded.

"No one. Ruby is going to go get the truck and bring it here as soon as I know you have my money," he said, calm as could be.

He amazed her. She could tell he wasn't playing any role right now. He was Damon Colton, not Damon Jones. Santiago wouldn't know that, though. That was when Ruby realized Damon had not really been faking it the whole time. For the most part, his confident personality drove his character as a bartender looking to make some illegal cash.

"I need to see the guns before I give you the cash," Santiago said.

Orlando stepped forward, holding his weapon aimed at the ground—for now.

"Show me the cash, and then we'll bring the guns," Damon said, clearly not afraid. His entire demeanor was daunting. Ruby marveled over that. He was such a man.

She saw Santiago take note of that. Damon would not back down. If he wanted his guns, he'd do as Damon asked.

Santiago turned to Carl and gave a nod. Carl, the obedient dog he was, went to a black SUV with dark-tinted windows. At the back, he withdrew a duffel bag. Returning to the group, he dropped it on the ground, then unzipped the top, jerking the opening wide to reveal an impressive pile of money.

Damon stepped forward and crouched, examining the bundles, fanning a few of them to make sure they were not counterfeit. Appearing satisfied, he stood and looked at Ruby. This was her cue to go get the truck.

She went to the car and drove the two blocks to where the agents had left the truck full of weapons. She saw an agent sitting on a bus-stop bench. She only knew he was an agent because Damon had told her he'd be there. His presence gave her some reassurance.

There were more agents surrounding the drop site, but she didn't see them. They were experts at covert operations. She began to feel empowered, part of something big and dangerous, with the law on her side.

Driving slowly, she turned into the alley behind the club. The group of men waited and watched her approach. Damon and his commander told her to wait in the truck.

Damon led Santiago and his men to the back of the truck, where he opened the door to show them the contents. Carl carried the bag of money.

Ruby could see a little of what transpired back there in the outside rearview mirror. She could hear Santiago's pleased voice.

"Good work, Damon. I think you'll fit right in," he said.

Damon moved to shake Santiago's hand, and she could now see his back. Carl handed him the bag of money. As soon as that happened, chaos erupted.

DEA agents poured out of buildings and into the open from every angle, guns aimed. They came from the back door of the nightclub, from around corners of buildings and into the alley. Ruby saw a sniper on the roof of a four-story building behind the club.

In the outside mirror of the truck, Ruby watched Santiago and his men glance around in shock. Then Santiago turned to Damon. "You son of a bitch."

To her horror, he took out a gun and fired. Damon flew backward and landed on the ground.

A sniper's shot hit Santiago in the head. His body collapsed to the ground.

Santiago's men began firing at agents.

Gunshots rang out. Worried sick about Damon,

Ruby ducked down in the truck as the volley of shots continued for endless seconds.

Then the shots quieted, and all Ruby heard were agents yelling for Santiago's men to drop their weapons. She sat up and looked around. Agents passed the truck and ordered Santiago's men on the ground with their hands up.

As soon as she knew it was safe, Ruby got out of the truck and ran to Damon, kneeling by his side. He grimaced in pain and held his shoulder.

"Let me see."

He moved his hand, full of blood. More blood drained from the wound.

"Oh." Urgency overtook Ruby. The shot was too high to have damaged any organs, but he was bleeding badly.

She ripped his shirt to expose the wound and checked for an exit. There was one. There was no bullet left in his body.

A man with a DEA Agent jacket on knelt beside her. "I'm a paramedic."

Ruby gave him room but stayed near Damon. He dug into his backpack and produced a bandage.

Ruby took it from him and applied pressure while the paramedic secured it with tape, tightly to stop the bleeding.

"You a nurse?" the paramedic asked.

"I will be, as soon as I finish school," she said.

"She's a nurse," Damon said. "And I'm her first patient." Damon grinned and all but stopped Ruby's heart. How could he smile at a time like this? A moment later, she had her answer. This was Damon

Colton. DEA agent. Brave. Handsome. But most of all, a hero.

Ruby looked down at Damon, meeting his eyes, secure with the sense that he was going to be all right.

"You're so beautiful," he said.

"You're just saying that because you've lost too much blood."

He chuckled, then winced.

Ruby kept pressure on his wound. "Sorry. A nurse shouldn't joke at a time like this."

"I'll get an ambulance," the paramedic said. He stood and rushed off.

Looking from his departure to Damon again, she touched his cheek, and they shared warmth in the intangible feelings they had for each other. Ruby appreciated his ability to rise above the pain he must be in.

Hearing someone approach, she assumed it was the paramedic, but instead it was a six-foot man with close-cropped medium-brown hair and beard. His green eyes with a grayish tint were serious. Ruby recognized him through her association with Sean. He was Harry Cartwright, a detective with the Chicago PD.

"Is he all right?"

"He's going to be," Ruby said. "The shot went through his shoulder."

The ambulance arrived, and Ruby stood.

Damon winced in pain as he was moved onto a gurney.

Ruby put her hand on his chest. "I'll follow you to the hospital." Leaning over, she kissed him briefly.

His expression smoothed, a fleeting alleviation of pain that put a grin on his mouth.

Always a gentleman, maybe a ladies' man. He had a pure soul. She squeezed his hand before he was rolled away, seeing him meet her gaze until she couldn't see him anymore. "Seems I have some catching up to do," Harry said.

Ruby turned to him, wondering at first what he meant and then catching on. He could tell she and Damon had more going on than the Mercer investigation. With a beard that only just covered his skin around his mouth and chin, his eyes held the somber resolve of a devoted detective. She saw the same in Damon. She checked his ring finger and found it bare of jewelry. She found it odd— or maybe unfortunate— that he hadn't found a woman to share his life with. But then...neither had she. People had reasons for not diving into relationships.

"You know Damon?" she asked.

He nodded. "I work in Narcotics. Yes, I know him, and I was part of this task force."

"Working in the background?" Not having to lie...

"Yes. I suppose you can say that. Damon had to be undercover, as I'm sure you can understand."

She did. Damon could not reveal his identity. Doing so would have put his life at risk. Even Ruby had to admit he had done what he had to do with her. They hadn't known each other. He couldn't trust her as a stranger. As hurt as she was by his betrayal, she did understand. But she still had to get past the hurt. Emotions didn't come with conditions. They were felt, and humans had to come to terms with them. In some way.

Harry eyed her speculatively. "Or maybe you don't."

Ruby bowed her head, self-conscious at her transparency. Then she met Harry's eyes. "I met Damon as a bartender. I didn't know he was a DEA agent."

Harry took some time before he replied. He seemed to assess her and her connection to Damon.

"I've been on the periphery of this investigation. Working behind the scenes, as it were. But from what little I've seen of the two of you, I'd have to say Damon's cover ID doesn't matter all that much."

His insight both speared her with fright for the state of her heart and hope for a fairy-tale future. "You seem like a nice man, Mr. Cartwright."

"Harry."

"Harry. Thank you for telling me what you did." She meant it. He had eased her mind over what had tormented her and continued to do so. She wasn't sure if she could overcome all she'd been through because of Damon and his investigation. Granted, he had saved her from the aftermath of Kid, but he wasn't the man she'd met that first time he bought coffee.

"Damon is a very lucky man," Harry said.

Lucky? How?

"You got away from a very dangerous man," Harry said, as though reading her thoughts. Maybe he had. Maybe he had picked up on something in her eyes.

"You got your daughter back, and you helped us take down the rest of Kid's organization," Harry said.

He made her feel important, as though she had played a key role in the investigation. Maybe she had.

Yes, she had. Without her, Santiago and his men would not have been stopped. She would have been haunted the rest of her life.

"I..." She didn't know what to say. *Thank you* seemed inadequate.

No problem...

"Hey, just living my life and trying to protect my daughter..."

Looking for love...

Harry chuckled. "I can see why Damon is so captivated by you."

"Oh... I..." He was making her so uncomfortable.

Harry chuckled again. "Sorry. I just want to thank you. A lot of people worked very hard bringing Kid's organization down, and it couldn't have been done without you."

"Oh..." She knew that to be true, but she didn't know how to respond. She didn't feel instrumental. She felt like more of a victim.

"I... I need to get to the hospital."

"I have a car for you. Come with me."

As she followed Harry, she contemplated his insight, whether he had planned to provide it or not. He'd told the truth, that's all, and she struggled with what that meant for her and Maya's future. Kid was permanently gone from their lives. None of his followers would pose a threat to her and Maya anymore. To be released from that felt...surreal. She had lived in fear for so many years, to finally be free of that—of Kid—felt so abrupt. But she was free. Maybe she just needed some time to adjust.

Damon.

Now that his investigation was over, what would he do? With the absence of excitement, would he still want her? How would their relationship change?

Ruby dreamed of having a family: mom, dad and daughter. A playset in the backyard. A barbecue. A home full of homeyness. Was that possible with a federal agent?

She didn't want any excitement beyond school activities and community participation. Neighborhood friends. Would Damon be happy with that?

Damon was more like Ruby and reluctant to form casual relationships. More and more she had to face the fact that they might be meant for each other. She was still too afraid to let go, at least not completely. She'd been burned before. She would not be burned again.

Chapter 16

Ruby paced the waiting area at the hospital. She bit her thumbnail. She folded her arms. Damon's team was busy processing the arrests of Kid's men and the death of Santiago. She was alone. She had decided not to call January yet. She didn't want to alarm Maya.

Finally, a doctor approached.

"Ruby Duarte?"

"Yes." Her heart raced with apprehension. Nothing mattered more than Damon right now.

"Damon is going to be all right."

Ruby took a few deep breaths, closing her eyes.

"We did surgery on the wound, and he should have a full recovery," the doctor said.

She tipped her head back. "Oh. That's wonderful to hear."

The doctor smiled, flashing not teeth but fondness. "He's demanding to see you. He's been quite the uncooperative patient ever since he woke from anesthesia."

She breathed a laugh. "That sounds like Damon." Damon needed to be in control, fighting for justice.

"Come with me." The doctor wore a slight grin as he led her to the elevators. They rode up a few seconds before the doctor said, "Congratulations, by the way."

She looked at him. "Pardon me?"

"Damon said you two are getting married."

Married? Why had he said that to the doctor?

"What kind of drugs did you give him?" she asked.

The doctor chuckled. "The kind to make some people honest. Although, his confession did seem genuine, like he'd say it without being in pain and on meds."

Ruby was speechless. Damon had professed marriage to strangers. Had he lost his mind? No. Drugs. That had to be it. Or was it…?

"I don't normally reveal things like that to those who aren't my patients, but he told me about you and how he feared you'd never trust him."

When she turned shocked eyes to him, he said, "That's all I can say. He told me a lot more, but I risk my medical license telling you what I have already. I did so because I believe it's worth it."

Numbly, Ruby nodded. "I understand, and…thank you." The doctor had clearly seen something special in Damon and his feelings for Ruby. Why else would he go out of his way to make her understand?

He extended his arm.

Ruby realized they were at the door of Damon's room.

She entered and heard the doctor close the door, no

doubt for privacy. She admired his discretion as much as his compassionate and interactive insight. He must have seen something in Damon that made him subtly intervene.

She stepped slowly toward Damon's hospital bed. He was slightly inclined, and his arm was in a sling.

Hearing her, he turned his head.

Ruby stopped. Even sleepy and wounded he was still so gorgeous and strong.

"The nurse taking care of me is completely inferior to you," he said.

She laughed, so glad he was all right. She went to the side of the bed, sitting on the edge and putting her hand on the side of his face.

"Did you meet Doc?" he asked.

"Yes."

"I think he is on my side."

"I think you have painkillers running through your veins. You told him too much."

She moved her hand to his chest, patting him a few gentle times.

"I told him the truth."

"Drugs cloud minds. Stop."

He put his hand over hers on his chest, the one that didn't have an IV in it. "Not when it comes to love, Ruby."

"You confided in a stranger," she said. But inside, her soul rejoiced. Dare she believe?

Damon sighed, tiredly. "I did."

His confession only dug deeper into her heart. He would be a permanent resident there if she wasn't careful. "I should let you get some sleep. I just wanted to make sure you were going to be okay."

"Are you trying to run away again, Ruby? Because if you are, you don't have to," he said.

Okay, he was being way too candid. "I should go." She started to get up, but he grasped her hand.

"Don't go," he said. "Stay with me."

"In the hospital?"

"No, forever."

"Damon..." She felt so flustered. Did he mean this? "Why?"

"Because you love me, too."

Unable to refute that, Ruby said nothing. And she was rescued when more visitors arrived.

January and Sean brought flowers and hugs. Damon's brothers visited for a bit. His cousins came as well.

Ruby was about to tell them all to go away and let him sleep, but Damon's spirits were so high she refrained. He loved family so much. It touched her heart in a way she had never experienced before.

A few minutes later, Damon's family began saying goodbye and filing out of the room. Next, in walked Damon's commander, Brian McNatt, a big man with dark brown hair and eyes that had seen too much. Damon had a busy room.

"Damon." Brian walked over to the bed. "How are you feeling?"

"They've got me comfortable. Keeping me overnight for observation."

"Good. You got lucky. It could have gone another way," he said.

Ruby was all too aware of that. If Santiago's aim had been better, she might be dealing with never seeing Damon again. The thought of losing him filled her with an awful feeling.

"Did you get all of Santiago's men?" Damon asked.

Not all of them had been present at the raid.

"We're rounding them up." Brian looked at Ruby. "If you need a safe place to stay, I can arrange that for you."

"She's going to stay with me," Damon said, then looked at her. "At my real home."

The way he said that warmed her through and through. What he hadn't said but she knew he meant for her to understand was he wanted her to know more about him, Damon Colton.

"All right," Brian said. "My main reason for coming here today is to commend you on a job well done. We couldn't have taken down Mercer's gang without you." He looked at Ruby. "You, too. The DEA thanks you both."

You're welcome didn't seem appropriate to Ruby, so she said nothing.

"Just doing my job," Damon said.

"I'll leave you two. Get some rest." Brian left.

Unfortunately, Damon would not be able to get rest. His next visitor was Harry.

"They said you were in Recovery," Harry said. He walked to the bed and took Damon's hand in a manly grasp. "How are you?"

"I'm fine."

"Hey, you did great back there. I wanted to personally tell you that, friend."

"Thanks. It's good to see you. Are you still with Narcotics?"

"Yeah."

"Maybe we could work together on a case sometime," Damon said.

"I'd be honored, but that won't happen. I've been promoted to head of Homicide."

"Really? That's great. Congratulations, man," Damon said.

Ruby listened to them talk about work. After about twenty minutes, Harry bade farewell and left.

"I heard he dated Carly Colton and he's a bit of a womanizer," Ruby said.

"He lost his wife and child to a murderer," Damon said. "He's got some issues from it."

That was terrible, but still, any woman who fell for him might lose her heart. Maybe that was Ruby talking from her own experiences, though.

"Better watch Lila. The last thing another Colton woman needs is to fall for him too much."

Damon chuckled. "Ruby, come here."

She did, and he took her hand and drew her closer. She leaned over as he put his hand behind her head and kissed her, long and slow. When he finally released her she was breathless and hot.

"You're lucky you're in this hospital bed," she said.

"More like unlucky," he said.

By evening the next day, Ruby drove Damon to his house. He gave her directions on the way. In a modern neighborhood, he had an average house that was clean and well maintained. Inside the entry, he saw her look around. The six-by-six-foot tiled entry branched off to the living room on the left, family room on the right, and an L-shaped stairway led to the upper level. He wasn't much of a decorator, so furniture and the modern architecture did the work for him.

She wandered through all the rooms on the first level, then went upstairs. He had three bedrooms up there. Plenty for the three of them. He tried not to hope too much.

Moments later she reappeared.

"The basement is partially finished," he said. "I want to make another master bedroom and a family room down there."

"It's nice, Damon."

She seemed guarded again, as she always was when something struck her as genuine—when it came to him. Hope grew too strong, and she resisted.

"We should get you settled in." She put down her overnight bag.

"I can sit on the couch." His shoulder hurt, but he wasn't an invalid. "Let's order delivery."

"I can make dinner," she said.

"We've been through enough, don't you think? Let's relax tonight."

She smiled slightly. "Pizza and wings?"

"Loaded?" he asked. "A Supreme with everything on it?"

"Yes. Screw the calorie counting worries tonight. I'm starving."

"No anchovies, though."

"Yuck. No. Meat and lots of peppers, onions and mushrooms."

"Extra cheese and tomatoes."

Ruby took out her cell phone. "A man after my heart."

They liked the same kind of pizza. What more of a sign did they need to be convinced they belonged together?

Damon wasn't under any illusions, however. Ruby wasn't ready to give herself to him completely. He fully expected her to tell him they should take things slow. He had known that about her shortly after meeting her. Wasn't that one of the reasons why he had taken so long to take her out on a date?

He had to respect her for that. After his bout with a deceitful woman, he could take all the time necessary to secure a healthy relationship with Ruby. But that didn't mean he wouldn't try to convince her to live with him.

She ordered their meal and then looked around as though uncertain what to do next.

"There's some chilled wine in the refrigerator," he said.

"Do you want a glass?"

"My pain medication is enough. You should have one, though," he said.

"Is it that obvious that I don't know what to do with myself?" she asked with a smile.

"Yes, Ruby. I've told you before that you're transparent. Get some wine, and come here and sit with me."

She looked at him a moment as though contemplating what sitting close to him would lead to. Sipping some wine.

He chuckled. “There’s no way I’ll be able to make love. You’re safe.”

She laughed lightly. “You seem to know me so well.”

“I do.”

Seeming a little bashful or uncertain, she went to rummage up a wineglass. While she proceeded to uncork the wine and pour herself a moderate helping, he found an old family movie, something calming. Then she came over to the couch and sat beside him on his uninjured side.

Hiding a grimace, he put his arm across the back of the couch, and she snuggled in, curling up her legs.

He remained with her like that a while, not really paying attention to the television. He suspected she wasn’t, either. This was the first time they were both truly free of Kid Mercer’s bad influence. He wanted to begin getting Ruby thinking about their future.

“Now that our lives are back to normal, we can start fresh,” he said, waiting to see how she’d react.

“Normal,” she murmured and took another sip. “I can’t remember what that is anymore.”

Disenchantment had a way of doing that to a person. The bliss of innocence faded with life experiences. He used to have that attitude.

“I couldn’t, either, before I met you,” he said. “Meeting you has given me a whole new outlook.”

She tipped her head to look at him.

He could see she was trying to gauge whether to believe him or not. “Don’t worry.” He rubbed her arm. “I know you need some time. But I would like you to stay here with me. You and Maya.”

She rested her head on his shoulder. "I'm not sure about that, Damon."

"I know. All I'm asking is you give me a chance to earn your trust. The investigation is over. You have me to yourself now."

"Until your next investigation?" she said.

"You won't be involved in that. You'll be safe."

After a while she sighed. "My lease is up at my house at the end of this month."

Damon felt that was a stroke of luck for him. "Then, it's decided. You, Maya and your mother—if she wants to—can come and live here."

Ruby moved to sit up, putting her glass on the coffee table. Then she angled herself to face him, clasping her hands on her lap.

He knew what she was going to say before she spoke.

"I'm not quite ready for that. With all that's happened, being reunited with Maya so recently, and surviving the aftermath of Kid. And…you… I…"

Damon reached to put his hand over hers. "It's all right, Ruby. I have a suggestion."

She met his eyes, listening and interested.

"Nicole came to see me when you went down to the cafeteria before I was released. She asked about us, and I told her everything. She offered for you to come and stay with her. You, Maya and your mother. She has plenty of room, and she'd love the company. Apparently you made quite an impression on her." His mother had told him if Ruby needed space after all she'd been through that she should stay with her. She wanted to help Damon keep her in his life.

A soft smile emerged on Ruby's beautiful face. She was more than physically beautiful. She had an inner glow, a purity about her. More than ever Damon wanted her in his life.

"And we can date?" she asked.

"You'll see me every day, sweetheart. We just won't be sleeping together. The DEA is going to give me a lot of time off."

He sensed her weighing her options. His no-pressure approach appeared to be working. He grew encouraged.

"Nicole said she would help watch Maya while you went to school. She's excited about having a child in her life. She's a really great mother figure."

Again, he sensed Ruby contemplating all he said.

"You won't have to work anymore until you graduate," he said.

She turned to look at him again.

"Just say yes, Ruby," he said.

With a big smile, she said, "Yes."

The ring of his cell phone interrupted. He winced as he moved to get it from his back pocket. Seeing it was Erik, he wasn't surprised the man had ruined a good moment with Ruby.

"Dad?"

"Hello, son. I heard what happened and wanted to call and see how you were doing."

Erik never showed signs of concern toward him. This was highly unusual.

"I'm recovering fine."

"Good. Good." He cleared his throat. "I also wanted to apologize for barging in on you at the barbecue."

Erik Colton…*apologizing?*

"That was a little dramatic. Are you sure you want to pursue that lawsuit?" Damon asked, wondering if the question would incite Erik's notorious temper.

Erik sighed. "It wasn't my decision to dispute the will."

"No, it was Grandmother's. That doesn't mean you and Axel have to support it," Damon said.

"It's too late to back down now. Can you just go along with it?"

So, that was the real reason Erik had called. Maybe he had genuinely wanted to make sure his son was all right, but he'd used the opportunity to his advantage.

"Why can't you stand up to her? You and Axel both."

"It's not about standing up to her, son. She does have a valid point that my brother and I deserve to at least be recognized as part of Dad's family."

"You'll destroy our cousins' lives if you win the lawsuit," Damon said.

Erik didn't respond. "I don't want to destroy anyone's life, Damon, but Mother has a right to claim what belongs to us. And like I said, Axel and I can't back off now."

Then, there was nothing else he had to say to his father. "I get it. Thanks for calling."

"I wish you could understand," Erik said.

"I do." More than he could possibly comprehend, having been molded from childhood by Carin.

"I'll check in on you in a few days," Erik said.

And Damon gladly ended the call.

Chapter 17

Ruby stayed with Damon until Brian told them all of Kid's criminal associates were now in jail awaiting trial. Damon made it easy for her to agree to live with Nicole for a while. She had spoken with her mother, who had decided to live with Ruby's sister. She missed Wisconsin and promised to come visit often. Ruby had been saddened by the news. She had grown accustomed to having her mother around all the time, but she understood. There were things she missed about Wisconsin, too.

Come to think of it, her mother had likely come to stay with her because of all she'd been through. In their last conversation, she told Ruby how happy she was for her, meaning that she had found Damon. Her mother felt all right about leaving her, returning to her hometown.

She turned from the lovely view of manicured landscaping to find Nicole approaching.

"Maya loves her room," Nicole said.

Nicole had told her she had redecorated one of the bedrooms, one right next to where Ruby would stay. And one of her help had taken Maya there.

"You shouldn't have done that. You're spoiling her."

"Not that much." Nicole took her hand. "You haven't seen it yet. Come with me."

Ruby began to feel that familiar defense swell. "I'll tuck my own daughter into bed." She had spent too many years without hugs and *I love you*s. People needed affection. Kids needed that even more. In dysfunctional environments, kids didn't get enough hugs and *I love you*s. Ruby would not tolerate anyone out of line with that.

"Oh." Nicole stopped. "Ruby, I meant no harm. Just come and see."

Ruby went with her, feeling a strange sense of trust, despite the fact that she didn't really know the woman Damon called Mom.

At the door of Maya's room, Nicole stepped aside so Ruby could see inside.

Soft lights and color took Ruby's breath away. Stars rotated on the ceiling. Flowing, silky drapes covered tall windows, and there was a canopy bed befitting Cinderella.

But what truly captured her was Maya in front of a lighted dollhouse. A huge one. She was immersed in a fairy-tale, dreamlike state.

"Ni—"

"Nope," Nicole cut her off in a soft tone. "Let her."

Let her...

Ruby's entire being shifted and tingled with newfound love.

"You deserve this," Nicole said. "You deserve it like Damon and Nash deserved a real home."

Her words hit her on impact. Ruby turned before Maya could see her and went into her room, sitting on the bed and breaking down into a torrent of tears. It was as though all the trauma she'd endured flowed out of her now that the threat had vanished. An emotional release. Like a war veteran, only they were so fortunate to find their way to any kind of release.

Ruby felt like a war veteran.

Surrounded by people who offered love and support, she breached a wall that had protected her for years. It fell. It crumbled. What was left was new hope for a happy future. With Damon. With his brothers and Nicole and aunts and cousins. Everyone. With her family.

Family.

Nicole sat beside her, careful not to infringe on her space.

Ruby cried harder and turned to bury herself against Nicole, soaking up the comfort freely offered.

Maya tugged hard on her shirt.

The urgency brought Ruby's immediate attention. Nicole moved away.

Ruby crouched to her daughter and took her into her arms. Leaning back she signed, *Mommy's fine, baby. We're with family now.*

Maya smiled and relaxed, signing, *Where is my new dad?*

He's not your new dad yet, Maya.

Yes, he is.

Do you know what weddings are?

Maya's perplexed look gave her the answer.

You've seen them in your cartoons. It's when a man and a woman, meaning me and Damon, get married. We dress up nice and pledge our love for each other. That's a wedding.

Maya's adorably innocent, young eyes met hers as she digested that.

If that happens with me and Damon, then he will be your new dad, Ruby signed.

After continuing to think over what Ruby said, Maya signed, *Then, you have to have a wedding with him.*

Ruby smiled, bursting with love, and pecked a kiss on the tip of her tiny, soft nose.

"That's a lovely thought, Maya." She signed as well.

For the first time since before she'd met Kid, Ruby felt safe pondering a future with a man.

Damon planned a few dates with Ruby and some time at home with Maya. Today it was Picnic Day. He took them to a park with a playground. He'd been taking it slow with her for over a week now.

Maya occupied herself on the slide while Ruby and Damon set up a picnic table with their lunch.

"I could get used to this," Damon said. "Outings with my family."

With his smile, she lowered her gaze and finished fixing Maya a peanut butter and jelly sandwich. She added some cheddar flavored chips to a plate and then waved to her daughter, catching her attention.

Maya came to the table and sat before her plate, digging in.

Ruby made Damon and herself turkey sandwiches and dished out potato salad and coleslaw. He popped open three sodas, giving one to Maya.

Handing him a plate, Ruby began eating, looking at Maya and then out across the park.

"Do you trust me yet?" Damon kept asking her that, mostly teasing, but today he was serious.

She turned to him. "A little bit more every day."

Her soft tone told him she had given him an honest answer. "I can't ask for more than that. But it's time I told you something."

He put his hand over hers on the table. He wanted her to pay close attention.

She waited, but he saw that she had stiffened almost imperceptibly. She expected him to reveal something else he hadn't told her.

"I'm not going anywhere, Ruby," he said.

She angled her head slightly in misunderstanding.

"I'm going to keep coming around as often as possible—with your permission, of course. And I don't care how long it takes for you to be completely and totally comfortable with me and trust me when I say I love you."

Her mouth dropped open a bit, and her eyes became acutely alert.

"Yes. I love you, Ruby. I'm certain of it. No matter what happens, no matter what you ultimately decide, I won't have any regrets. I love you like no other woman, so if you won't have me, I'll let you go with the hopes that you will find happiness with someone else. No regrets."

Now she appeared stunned into silence.

"You can take as long as you need to feel safe with me. For your heart to feel safe in my hands and my love. I'll wait as long as it takes. The important thing for you to know is I'm not going anywhere. I won't give up on you. Not ever. Until you tell me you want me to go and I believe you."

It was the most heartfelt confession he had ever made to anyone. He was risking everything with her right now. But she was worth it. She was a hundred times the woman his fiancée had been.

After several moments, tears brimmed in Ruby's eyes. "You have no idea what that means to me."

"No, I don't, and I'd like for you to tell me."

She put her other hand over his. "Damon, my heart screams out that you are trustworthy despite all the deception." She lowered her head as she gathered her thoughts and chose words. "But in my mind… I…have trouble. All that I've been through."

"I know, Ruby. That's why you have all the time you need. I want you. I want to marry you and be a father to Maya. I want us to be a family. For real."

A tear slipped down her cheek. "Damon, I want that, too."

Joy swelled within him. They were going to be all right. She was going to be his wife…someday.

He caught Maya staring at them. She had likely read most of what they said.

She looked at him and signed, *My new daddy.*

* * * * *

Don't miss the next thrilling story in
Colton 911: Chicago:

Colton 911: Forged in Fire *by Linda Warren*

Available from Harlequin Romantic Suspense!

SPECIAL EXCERPT FROM

HARLEQUIN

ROMANTIC SUSPENSE

Former FBI and current undercover agent Luther Darby needs linguist Kit Danilenko's talents to bring down Russian Organized Crime in Silver Valley, and Kit needs Luther's law enforcement expertise. Neither wants any part of their sizzling attraction, especially when it becomes a liability against the two most powerful ROC operatives.

Read on for a sneak preview of
Stalked in Silver Valley,
the latest book in the
Silver Valley P.D. miniseries by Geri Krotow.

"Kit, you misunderstood me. Let me try again."

He saw her shake her head vigorously in his peripheral vision. If he could grab her hand, look her in the eyes, he would. So that she'd see his sincerity. But they'd started to climb and the highway had gone down to two lanes, winding around the first cluster of mountain foothills.

"No need. Just take me back home." This version of Kit was not the woman who'd greeted him this morning. Great, just great. It'd taken him, what, fifteen minutes to make mincemeat of her self-confidence? He felt like the lowest bird on the food chain, unable to escape the raptor that was his big mouth.

HRSEXP0921

"I'm not taking you home, Kit. We're going on this mission, together. I'm sorry if I pushed too hard on your history—it's none of my business. None of it." He needed to hear the words as much as say them. The reminder that she was a mob operative's spouse, albeit an ex, would keep him from seeing her as anything but his work colleague.

She was nothing like Evalina.

The memory of how the ROC mob honcho's wife had used him, how stupidly he'd fallen for her charms, made his self-disgust all the greater. It was one thing that he'd allowed himself to be duped and his heart dragged through the ROC crap. It was another to cause Kit, a true victim of her circumstances, any pain.

"Are you sure you can trust me, Luther?"

HRSEXP0921